SHADOWS FROM THE PAST

BY

GARY REICHERT

D1738089

PHOTO CREDIT:

clipartxtras.com

SHADOWS FROM THE PAST

The rain fell in sheets. Whatever progress that had been made on the road bed was beginning to erode. This would cause no end of regrading and repair, if the storm kept up its onslaught much longer. Crews had been let go for the day, so it would be tomorrow, at the earliest, before any damage repair could be made. That, of course, would depend upon the storm blowing on through.

The superintendent was still in the shack, studying the plans for crossing the pass and completing the series of culverts and bridges needed to span the numerous drainages on the mountain. He was suddenly disturbed by rustlings just outside of the project trailer. He had noted some noises about a half hour earlier, but stepping out to look had revealed nothing unusual. He ignored the sounds and continued his work. The rustling was augmented by some loud thumping and what sounded like branches breaking. Now that was new, and he opened the door to see just what had caused the ruckus.

The upper part of the mountain was bathed in alpenglow, but down the slope, where the trailer was parked, it was almost dark. Jake had heard something, but he had not recognized it as anything he was familiar with. He stepped out into the rain and gloom and peered into the nearby forest. He didn't know what to expect, but what he saw surely wasn't anything he had ever, in his wildest dreams, imagined. His eyes focused upon a beast, the like of which he had only seen in slick magazines and books or museums from a bygone era. His brain told him that it was impossible that such an animal could exist in this day and age. There was no way he could accept what he was looking at. He stared and then began to realize that the thing was indeed real and that it had seen him. That wasn't something he was prepared to accept, for several reasons. One was that he quickly became aware that the beast was snarling at him. Two was the sudden recognition that something else, very big and threatening, was very close behind him. A quick glance over his shoulder revealed another animal much like the first. But this one was much, much closer. Too damned close for sure. He was paralyzed by fear. He wanted to run, to hide, to disappear, but his mind realized that there wasn't anywhere close enough that was secure from these monsters. They were just too big. The trailer was no match for their size, that was evident to him.

He hadn't long to think about fleeing anyway. The beast behind him suddenly lurched forward and grabbed him in its jaws. The pain was intense, with an overwhelming pressure on his upper body, just before his ribs and lungs were broken and crushed. Death followed quickly.

The animal walked off into the gloom holding the superintendent's body sideways in his mouth. The other beast quickly crossed the opening and snatched at the body with its jaws. The man was ripped apart as the two animals began to feast, each growling and snapping at the other. It was now completely dark. The rain fell like a deluge. Then the roadbed began to wash. Blood ran in rivulets, joining the small streams of rainwater rushing down into the bar ditch. A half hour after the attack revealed very little that was once a man. The smaller forest creatures would scour the area for any leftovers by the two beasts. Only scraps of clothing, pocket items, and a watch would attest to what had once been a human.

The rain continued to pour down, washing out all tracks and evidence that something very untoward had occurred at the construction site. The animals faded into the darkness, and all was still.

Chapter 2

It was an outpost café situated on a secondary road with light travel. The locals ate their breakfasts, served with plenty of pancakes, bacon or sausage, and heaps of scrambled eggs, family style. All you could eat was popular with regulars and tourists alike. The coffee was strong, and your cup was always filled.

The owner was a widow woman that was on the far side of fifty. Her name was Janey Smalley, and she had been tending to her restaurant for twenty years. The business had provided for her needs since her husband had gone missing during one of the hard winters that the country was noted for. He was later found in the spring at the bottom of a mountain side, where he had been buried under a snow avalanche. That had been fifteen years before. She had never re-married. There just wasn't much to choose from in her neck of the woods. So she decided to make the most of the business and serve folks good solid meals. In summer, the tourists added greatly to the profits but also to the extra work. She had hired two local girls to help out with the waitress duties. She cooked, cleaned, kept the books, ordered the supplies, and tended to her two dogs and three cats. The dogs made out OK, but the cats never seemed to last more than a few short years. There were just too many predators that were fond of cat meat. So Janey always had a momma cat around to re-supply the mousers, whenever they would be taken by an owl, an eagle or a coyote.

She was content to care for her pets and run the business. The remoteness of the location had no real appeal for Janey, but she had been left with the restaurant when her husband died, so she made the best of it. She had many friends though, and because of the sparse population and huge wildlands surrounding the area, she felt that the regulars at the café were like family. All had been going well these last few years, but for the occasional unexplained disappearance of someone. They just seemed to vanish into thin air. There had never been a reasonable solution to the missing persons that, from time to time, just ceased to be seen or heard from.

Some of the locals liked to blame the disappearances on Sasquatch, grizzly bears, serial killers, or abductions by aliens. None of those theories seemed to fit though. Most grizzly attacks didn't result in death and bodily disappearances. And grizzlies hibernated in the winter. Some of the missing person reports occurred in the dead of winter. Serial killers liked notoriety and the attention of the media. Sasquatch was fun and mysterious, but few people took it seriously. And then there was the always popular alien abduction and later confession by those abducted. There was just no good explanation for these strange events, which made them even more weird and terrifying.

The local Sheriff's Offices organized mounted patrols, helicopter searches, and dog units. The news people reported and speculated and advanced theory upon theory. They regularly left after the expected three days of panic, mystery, and finger pointing. And they came back again for the typical media circus, whenever another victim vanished into the gloom and the eerie stands of spruce, fir, and lodgepole. Those were the forests that covered several thousand square miles of northwestern Montana, Idaho, and Washington. So the mystery continued and grew, and some folks moved away from that wet, dank forest, never to return.

Janey was as mystified as anyone, but she didn't dwell on the theories, and she didn't engage in gruesome speculation. She figured that whatever the explanations for the events, speculation didn't matter much to her. She paid attention to her friends and neighbors, ran the café, and tried to live her life in a stable, useful manner. And, she hoped for the best, because the alternative frightened her, badly. The mystery was palpable, and Janey was not the only local scared by it. There were many others.

Chapter 3

The road crew hustled into the warmth of the café as morning tried to break through the clouds. It had failed once again. The steady downpour held off any sunlight that might possibly arrive through the trees.

There were thirteen of them, and they took up about a quarter of the tables and booths in her place. The waitresses brought water and menus, poured coffee, and took orders for pancakes, eggs, bacon, and ham. Janey got to work on the breakfasts.

Another group, a half-dozen locals, bumped and stomped their way into the place and ordered coffee and sweet rolls. They became somewhat subdued once they sat down. They looked the road crew over with distain and obvious superiority and then completely ignored them. Outsiders were tolerated but were not really welcomed around their neck of the woods.

But the locals changed their minds and attitudes when two more road crew members entered the café. They were dyed blond, attractive women in their early thirties. They filled out their pants and shirts in a way that got lingering looks from most any man in the place. The mood seemed to lighten within the room. The locals reconsidered. Maybe they had been a bit hasty in their judgment of the outsiders. Maybe they should be a little friendlier to strangers. It was something to ponder.

The women took seats at the tables occupied by their fellow construction workers. The talk picked up and soon became a real din. The waitresses arrived with platters of food, and the talk fell off to a low rumble as the road crew dug into breakfast. Coffee cups were topped, and all was right with the world.

One of the road crew members, Jimmy Bench, asked the others where Jake was. No one seemed to know. Jimmy said that Jake should have been here by now, if they were going to get anything done about work that morning. They all agreed, but no one ventured a guess as to what Jake was up to. He, as a habit, kept to himself when off duty. And it was common knowledge that he often worked late in the shack. There was always much to do as superintendent, ordering, coordinating, studying plans, and a myriad of other functions that combined to make the project roll on.

The road crew finished off their breakfast and began to fidget, waiting for Jake to appear in order to find out if they worked that day or not. So Jimmy called Jake's cell several times and got the voice message, but there was no pick up. The two blond women were enjoying the attention of most of the male counterparts of the road crew. And the girls had also noted the apparent interest of a couple of the locals, seated in the far corner of the room.

Time passed, and Jake didn't show. So Jimmy Bench called over to Janey Smalley about Jake's no-show. She came right to the table to find out what they were concerned about. Jimmy asked her if she had seen Jake last night.

"You know, Jake is a regular for all meals, but he never came in last night. I thought that a bit unusual, but I know how late he often works, so I really didn't think too much about his not showing up last evening. But not having him here for breakfast is beginning to cause me some concern about his whereabouts. Maybe you people should go out to the site and look him up. I am beginning to feel kind of worried about him. Would you do that?"

"You bet we will. We need to get to work, if we can, and Jake is the only one that can give the go ahead, if we are going to get busy today or not. OK, so we'll check it out and give you a call, Janey. Let's get going, people."

The road crew trooped out, got into their trucks, and headed off to the site. The rain had dropped off to a fine mist. Low, hanging clouds swirled around the tops of the trees that continued to drip moisture. All was green and clean and cool.

Very little evidence awaited the road crew as to what had befallen Jake. And that little evidence was fast disappearing due to magpies, Clark's nutcrackers, rodents, and even some ants that had arrived to work over the scraps of meat and skin that had once been Jake Andersen.

The construction trucks arrived twenty minutes after leaving the restaurant. Jake's truck was still parked in the same place that it had been the day before. The keys were in the ignition. Several of the men checked on it while the rest of the crew entered the trailer. There was no sign of Jake except for his calculator, architect's rule, cell phone, and writing pad. The coffee pot was half full and completely cold. His coat hung on the back of the chair. The shack was still and quiet, obviously deserted. The crew was puzzled and some of them scared.

The D-9 operator, Ben Garza, began to get the creeps. And he apparently wasn't the only one. Both women were showing too much white around the eyes. Several of the other men began a furtive glancing around, seeing nothing. The up-beat morning mood had dissipated and had been replaced with a certain grim foreboding.

"What the hell is going on around here? Where the hell did Jake get off to? This is beginning to look awfully weird to me. This is totally not like Jake. Something is really, really, wrong, and I for one am not about to pass it off. Damn it, people, what should we do? There is no sign of him anywhere around here. I guess that nothing's left to do, and unless someone has another idea, I'm calling the cops right now." Ben was speaking for all of them. They needed to move, do something, and calling the cops was the best and the first good idea that anyone had had.

Ben dialed 911 and waited. It took a while for the dispatcher to answer, but eventually she did.

"Look, lady, I'm calling to report a missing person. I am a heavy equipment operator with the construction crew, working up on the flank of Boundary Peak. Our superintendent, Jake Andersen, failed to come off the mountain last night. His truck is still parked where it was yesterday, with the keys in the ignition. There is no sign of him at the construction shack. We haven't seen anything that looks like someone else came after we all left, early yesterday afternoon. This isn't like Jake. He would never abandon his job. He is the most conscionable, careful, and reliable person that I've ever known. I hope you can get someone up here fast, because we are at a total loss to explain this."

The call went out to all of the jurisdictions in a three-state area. Many of those receiving the call felt a familiar chill run down their spines. They had been involved in other strange, missing person events. In the searching, the guessing, the shifting of blame, the media made law enforcement look incompetent and foolish, like a bunch of uneducated hillbillies. Now here it was about to begin all over again.

One of those men, that had worked several disappearances over the years, was Lincoln County deputy Wade Larson. Larson was a twenty-year man with the Sheriff's Office. A very sharp sergeant, who was more than familiar with strange disappearances. He had a particular interest in these occurrences and had been putting together any and all evidence, reports, false alarms, and cold case files. His only nephew had vanished not three years ago, without a trace. It had happened on an adjacent mountain next to Boundary. The call, just now, had brought back all of the frustration, fear, anger, and helplessness that he had experienced when Billy had disappeared. Wade's sister had wallowed in grief right up to the present day. Her husband had finally had enough and had packed up and left her. Wade would never forgive him for that brutal move, but the fact that he considered the offending husband "a piece of shit" helped to ease some of the anger he felt.

The Lincoln County Sheriff, Jefferson McDougal, got on the horn and began to line up search and rescue. He made the calls to the other jurisdictions, called old Willie Von Vorhees, and told him to ready his dogs. And he made sure that the mounted posse was notified.

Jimmy Bench called Janey Smalley with the report from the construction trailer. He told her about the call to 911 and that they would wait for the cops to arrive out at the site.

Janey's face blanched when she heard the news. Her heart began to beat faster, and she felt like she was going to faint. It had happened again. She knew it the minute the construction crew began to ask her about Jake. It was the nightmare come true once more, and it would stalk her life for many, many nights to come. Suddenly it felt very cold in the restaurant. She pulled on a sweater, poured a cup of coffee, and sat down at the eating bar, resting her head in her hands. Janey began to shiver.

Chapter 4

The ground was soaked from all of the rain. It should have been enough to cause animal tracks to remain wherever one had passed. But the problem with the heavy forest growth was that most of the ground was carpeted with inches thick, layers upon layers, of needles. There was a perfect mat of them. It tended to spread out the results of something walking across the mat, not leaving any actual identifying prints. As soon as the surface dried, it would spring back up and erase any evidence of passage. The situation for any tracker was compounded by the unknown fact that these particular beasts had very wide paws that spread out their weight and that they had retractable claws, leaving no nail prints at all.

Added to the ease with which these beasts traversed country was the fact that, being nocturnal, they were practically invisible. And a tracker needed a starting point, some reference to the scene of the event, and a direction that something had traveled after doing whatever it had done. But there was absolutely nothing to aid a tracker. It was a dead end.

Von Vorhees let the dogs get a good smell of Jake's jacket. Then he let them go. After an hour or so, he locked them back up. They had nothing. Oh, they had found a couple scraps of clothing pieces, but the trail was non-existent. Whatever had happened to Jake Andersen had happened right at the trailer. There was no scent of him beyond the immediate vicinity of the construction shack.

"I'm sorry, Sheriff, but the damned rain has washed out any potential scent, and the dogs are without a lead. I'm headed for the barn. If you need me, if anything comes up, you know the number."

Von Vorhees turned the flatbed around and rolled off downhill, leaving the construction crew, the sheriff and his deputy, and a couple of locals that had followed the hound man up the mountain. Talk centered on the fact that Jake, or more likely Jake's body, had completely vanished.

"Damn it to hell, Jefferson, it's just like what happened to my nephew. This situation gets weirder and spookier all the time. We are almost certain that none of the harped-on theories are worth a damn when it comes to these cases. There has to be some kind of clue to these disappearances that we are just flat-out missing. What is this, number six or seven? I can't remember any longer. How can something, or someone, just snatch a person right under our noses and leave no trace of him, or of themselves, or of it, whatever the hell it is? How can that be? Maybe we deserve to be called a bunch of dumb hillbillies out here, after all. The friggin' news media has us pegged pretty well, if we can't figure this out and put a stop to it."

"I know, Wade. Not only are we sure to be the butt of the jokes and criticism, we may have to deal with national media this time. That was the threat from the local affiliate, the last time we failed to come up with anything. But the media is the least of our concerns right now. We have something loose in our bailiwick, something that is killing people and hauling the bodies off to God-knows-where, and it just has to be stopped. What little population we have left up in this corner of the country is liable to pack it in and haul ass outa here, after this becomes public knowledge."

The sheriff went into the shack and made a pot of coffee. He knew that search and rescue and the mounted posse were getting their stuff together, but it was bound to be awhile before they showed up on the mountain. There was no sense in calling out a chopper, because the trees were just too thick for a helicopter to be of any use. So it would be a search the old-fashioned way. It was slow, but it could be fairly thorough for just that reason. Jefferson McDougal hated the mystery of the missing people. Not one bit of it made any sense, especially now that it was number seven. If he didn't know far better, he might believe that aliens had indeed descended and snatched these people off the earth. One thing that countermanded that was the four tiny scraps of Jake's Levi's found by the dogs. But the entire thing was damned strange. And it was pure lousy luck that the rain storm had washed away any chance for hound tracking.

The construction crew drove back down the mountain. Everyone was silent and morose. The two women were crying, and a couple of the guys had misty eyes. Jake had probably been the best boss anyone in the crew had ever had. He looked out for his people, but he never cut corners or allowed any slacking or fooling around. You put in a full day, every day, and you got paid, on time, every time. He had the full trust of the company, because he ran a tight ship. But the crew loved him, because he never acted like he was above them in any way. And, one thing was certain, Jake was smart, very smart. For the crew, it just didn't add up. Jake did not make mistakes. Something had come and had taken him away. Whatever it was, it was something that nobody in the crew could imagine. They had heard the stories of the disappearances when they first rented their motel. But they had passed the tale off as another attempt to scare off the newcomers by locals. Not anymore. This was as spooky as it got. And, until some kind of sense could be made of it, it would remain right at the top of their list of unimaginable, weird events in anyone's lifetime.

By the time the mounted posse got to the site, it was nearly four o'clock. They set a camp with several trailers, fed the horses, and got ready for supper. The light was fading fast. No search was about to commence this late in the afternoon. Tomorrow, at first light, they would ride off from the camp and begin to look in earnest for any sign, clue, or evidence that might be found. The search and rescue guys had arrived two hours earlier and had made a hasty search both north and south of the shack. Nothing had been found, and they returned around five o'clock to their camp. The hard work would begin on the morrow.

Chapter 5

The rain had begun again. It had turned off cold, gray, and miserable for anyone venturing out in it. It was a soaking, steady rain that penetrated to the marrow. The moss that covered the tree trunks, rocks, and downed logs thrived on it. The trees soaked it up, just before the later, brief, hot, summer sun could dry out the forest in preparation for the annual fires that raged through the canopy of lodgepole and fir. A few years after the fires, the new lodgepole pine would be four feet high and doghair thick. You could not walk through the new growth. But animals, particularly elk and/or moose, could navigate the miserable stuff with ease. For right now, the cold soaking rain was spreading its life-giving moisture to all of the vegetation and making everything and everybody else miserable.

Willie Von Vorhees had a feeling about the mystery and the problem. He also had some hard evidence that indicated a damned big animal had taken at least one of the missing people. He had never told a soul about it, but he guessed that an animal big enough to haul off a full-grown man had to be pretty damned stout.

A couple of years back Willie had stumbled upon something. He had kept it secret, hoping more evidence would finally show up. It never had, and he had scoured several square miles of mountainous terrain looking for it. He had put the dogs out, hoping for a trail, a print, or any other bone or bones. Nothing was all he had to show, except for the original discovery.

Willie had been crossing a narrow defile on the side of Northwest Peak, when he had literally kicked something buried in the creek grass underfoot. It was stained brown and covered in dirt, needles, and green moss. It was a human skull. The find was surprising but not all that unusual. Time to time, human remains were to be found in most any forest. A full skeleton was discovered in the Bitterroot Valley, after the infamous 2000 fires had burned over the brush and pine needles on a hillside. But Willie had a theory about his find because of some very interesting marks upon the skull. There was a deep groove, beginning above the left eye socket and running along the top of the skull to the back-side where it ended. The groove was very deep into the bone, and it was wide. It appeared to Willie that something with extra-large teeth had bitten down and dug a deep furrow in the victim's skull.

He had told no one and had never shown it to anyone either. There wasn't enough evidence to conclude what had happened. But Willie was giving it some serious thought now, since the disappearance of that construction fellow. The few scraps of Jake's clothing had convinced him that something very damned big was stalking around in his forest. Something that might possibly have something to do with the decline of the moose and elk in his neck of the woods. All of the locals had persisted with the theory that wolves were the culprits. That had held up with most of the general population of the local area. It was also convenient to blame wolves, the "friggin' federal government", the Indians, and the tree huggers for the depredations upon other wildlife. But old Willie had just changed his mind. He had remembered that the wolf population had also begun a steady decline some years back. The elk and moose should have bounced back when the wolves declined. That had not happened. Now he was almost certain that another factor was at work, but, so far, he had very little other than an idea. Not one shred of proof, except for the weird skull with the big tooth mark on it.

Willie had another problem with his theory. His dogs were very good on a trail. And they had never been able to find any kind of track or scent that they could follow. He knew that a lot of the problem was the rain that fell for days, washing out tracks and scent. So he hoped for a break, like maybe a long stretch of warm weather and sunlight that would spread across the forest. The dogs would eventually catch a scent, and off they would go. He just hoped that he would be capable of following up behind them, before they cornered whatever the hell the thing was. Any animal that left a bite mark, like the one on the skull, would surely make quick work of his dogs. Right about then, he made a resolution to begin carrying his .45-70 lever action carbine everywhere. It might make the difference on something big. There were a lot of shells up the spout of the old carbine. And he just might need every one of them, depending on whatever the hell was out there.

He had lived in these parts for sixty years and had heard and seen enough strange things to last four lifetimes. But the missing people could no longer be dismissed as coincidence.

Something was definitely taking them, of that he was certain. He decided to call Sheriff McDougal. He really should know about the skull. But Willie sure as hell hoped that the glory-hunting news media didn't get wind of that skull. That would blow up into wild speculation and more complaints against law enforcement. He decided he needed an early morning meeting with the sheriff, before the news media could drive up from Kalispell.

The Van Vorhees log cabin was far from any well-traveled road. Most of the locals knew its location, but they didn't advertise where he lived. It just wasn't anybody's business. He liked the solitude and the distance from other people. His closest neighbor was nine miles away on a dirt track, around the far side of the mountain. He had never been bothered by man nor beast, other than an occasional mountain lion that tried to get into the chicken coop, or a fall bear looking to fatten up on his bee hives.

Willie's cabin was without electricity. He had a propane range, refrigerator, and propane lights. The lights were dim, but they gave off enough to read by. Whenever he ventured out at night to check on something, he carried a Coleman lantern.

Suddenly his hounds had set up a din, barking and howling like they were on a hot scent. It snapped Willie back to the present. It was very unusual for his hounds to act up like that, and Willie determined to find out just what was causing it.

He fired up the Coleman, walked outside, and headed for the kennels. The dogs increased their barking and howling. He could see nothing unusual in the darkness. The dogs calmed down some when he got near. He talked to them and got them to quit their frenzy of barking. The rain was being pushed by the wind, which had just switched and had begun blowing out of the east. The hounds had settled down now that the wind had shifted. The fact that he had come out to see what had upset them gave them assurance that everything was OK. He didn't waste around long, once they got quiet, because the rain was beginning to soak him, right through his coat.

Taking one last look around and giving the dogs one last word, he headed for the cabin. It was pitch black, and the wind was in his face, blowing rain water into his eyes. He couldn't hear much either, because of the wind. But he did hear something, suddenly, and it wasn't like anything he had ever heard before. A low rumbling growl caused his glance to shift to the right. There, not twenty-five feet away, was an apparition the likes of which he had never laid eyes upon. The thing was huge, black as the night, with very, very long fangs and penetrating green eyes. It was crouched, with ears flattened alongside it huge broad head. Willie was transfixed. Then he heard something else. There was another rumbling growl from behind him, and it was very close, too. He swung the lantern around just in time to see an open mouth, with huge fangs, sailing through the air above him. The beast hit him like a freight train, snapping his spine instantly. Willie was dimly aware of hot breath and then the final crushing of his skull, as the horrid mouth closed over his face.

Chapter 6

The search and rescue men and women had begun their work an hour before the posse had mounted and rode off in a different direction. The sheriff joined the search and rescue group and was staying in contact with Wade Larson, who had brought his own horse and gear and was now a mile out from the trailer. Wade was leading the posse in a large round about, casting for tracks, a body, or anything else that would confirm the suspicions of just about everybody in the local area. Some folks were sure it was another alien abduction; some were certain it was a pack of wolves or a grizzly bear. All of the regular suspects, but lacking the usual theory about a serial killer. The small tatters of Jake's Levi's kind of ruled out a serial killer in most everyone's mind.

They rode on for hours, making ever-widening circles. In the afternoon, the posse took a break high up on a wind-swept ridge of the mountain. There were a few openings within the forest that afforded a good view of the surrounding mountains and valleys. The country was huge, steep, and rugged. And the human population was sparse, or non-existent, in most of Lincoln County. It was, in fact, a perfect place to lose a trail or to get lost yourself. There could have been any number of large animals traveling the country round about, and nobody would ever be the wiser. This rugged corner of the three states, right up against the Canadian border, was remote to the extreme.

Wade Larson was familiar with all of the facts and rumors about the place where he lived and worked. He was in a constant condition of being reminded about those facts, while he searched for clues. The memory of doing the exact same thing, less than three years ago, still haunted him. Somehow, this time, they must find out. They had to discover the reason why so many had disappeared. The horror had to be stopped. He set his jaw and gazed off into the blue haze surrounding the tops of the Cabinet Mountains. It looked like another rain storm was headed their way, and that would make their job almost impossible. The posse began to wend their way back down the mountain in defeat.

The search and rescue volunteers had similar luck as had the posse. They returned even sooner to their trucks and headed down the mountain to Janey Smalley's Country Café. Beer and pizza were ordered by all, and the search and rescue crew settled in for an evening of pool, country music, and speculation about the blanket of mystery that they were under.

An hour and a half later, the mounted posse pulled in with diesel pickup trucks and horse trailers. They were cold and wet and defeated likewise. Another round of beer and pizza was ordered. The posse members shed their wet hats and jackets and spread out among the tables. They yearned for a little leg room in order to stretch their tired muscles, after the long hours a-horseback.

Wade Larson's girlfriend had been on the posse ride with him. She was ten years his junior, blond and willowy, with bright blue eyes and a nice smile. The smile was a little wan at the moment, due to the adverse circumstances, but she was game for more of the same, if it was what was needed. No one really had much of an idea about what to do.

Larson and Sheriff McDougal huddled in a corner booth for a few minutes and compared fruitless notes on the afternoon and evening attempts to find something, anything that would help explain the situation. They were as glum as they were wet and tired. It looked like another dead end. They both felt the uselessness of their efforts, and that was damned frustrating. To add to their discouragement, it had just been announced on the evening news that another missing person had been reported. Now the damned media fools were bound to show up, tomorrow morning most likely. The sheriff began to mentally cast around for an excuse to be absent from the office, especially the first thing in the morning. He couldn't pass it off onto Larson because of that deputy's day off. The interview would have to be handled by someone else that was office bound, because the sheriff was determined not to be anywhere near where he could be questioned. He knew that he had some warrants that needed to be served in the south part of the county, so he made plans to do just that.

Janey Smalley had been doing a fair job of keeping the fear from overtaking her, but it was lingering very close to the surface, and she was afraid that, at any moment, she was going to lose that battle. The apprehension she was feeling was building up close to panic. She drew her third glass of "Moose Drool" of the evening. Everyone in the place was feeling some degree of fear, terror, horror, or anger about the situation. Whatever the thing was that was taking people right in her back yard, it was winning. It was just entirely too much for her to think about.

The Construction crew trooped into the café and grabbed up some seats. The two waitresses took their orders. More beer, for sure, and a variety of food items were written up and hung on the rotating stainless-steel wheel above the cook line. Janey got busy on the orders. Someone dropped coins in the juke box, and a steel guitar and bass blared into the room. A collection of oldies had been selected, and the gravelly voice of Cash rumbled through the "Orange Blossom Special "and "Folsom Prison Blues". Cash was followed by Creedence Clearwater Revival's greatest hits. More beer was served, and the mood changed for the better.

Wade Larson and his girl, Mandy, joined two other couples on the dance floor, doing the cowboy two-step. The rain continued to pelt the windows while some of the patrons played pool, and the rest relaxed to the music. There was nothing for it but more beer. The pressure of evil in the darkness was being held at bay by old music, alcohol, loud talking, and nervous energy. It all was bound to be a lost cause, especially in the morning. No one really wanted to leave the café that night, but it got late, and the party broke up. Everyone departed for their own place. The road crew had a fifteen-minute drive to their motel. Most of the locals didn't have far to go. The sheriff and the deputy had the longest drives, back to the county seat at Libby.

Wade dropped Mandy at her place, kissed her good night, and drove off to unload his horse at the stable. It would take him the better part of an hour to care for the horse, hang up the wet tack and blanket, park the trailer, and drive home. He was tired in more ways than one, and he was anticipating his coming days off more than usual. Wade really hoped he could get a decent night's sleep. But that was not to happen. It turned out to be a night filled with more dread and more nightmares. He couldn't shake the foreboding he felt. The beast was out there, and he felt like it was stalking him, personally.

Something was bound to break this time, he just knew it. But what, was the question. Wade had a friend that owned an African big game rifle. He intended to borrow that piece, first thing tomorrow. If whatever was taking these people was as big as he suspected, he would need something greater than his .300 Weatherby to take it down. Raymond Shelton owned a Winchester Super Grade in .458. He was going to buy plenty of ammo and get on the range tomorrow. It would take a bit to get used to the heavy recoil. But it would be worth the effort. The .458 was a damned elephant gun, and that ought to do the trick, if anything could. He got on the phone and lined it up with

Shelton that very night. Raymond Shelton, an old friend, had offered the gun anytime that Wade might need it, a couple of years back. Wade hadn't thought that he would ever need it, when he was looking for his nephew. But he had just changed his mind. This beast was strange and terrifying, and Wade felt that he really had a good reason for the larger caliber now. He was going to hunt this bastard down, if it was the last thing he ever did. And he thought it may well be the last thing. Wade figured to have the difference with the Winchester, if he ever got off a shot. That was a big question mark. What he was getting ready for was out of his league. Hunting dangerous game was really dangerous at best, but this thing, well, no one knew what the hell it was or what it was capable of. Wade took a quick shower and fell into bed, hoping for some shut eye.

 The morning finally came, after a long, long night. He got breakfast at the Old Libby Café, right downtown. He loved their special, real flapjacks. They just couldn't be beat. He washed it all down with plenty of strong coffee, left a good tip, and headed for Shelton's place to pick up the heavy weapon. Just the idea of that gun seemed to settle him down. A man needed to be ready when something untoward came. And he would be as ready as he had ever been, of that he was certain.

Raymond Shelton was a retired Baptist preacher. Originally from Texas, around San Antonio, he had migrated to Montana many years before. The .458 Winchester had served him fatefully on an African hunt some years before. He had actually bagged two Cape buffalo, a leopard, and a hippo with the heavy Winchester. When Shelton drew it out of the green felt, wooden case, it shone with a fine oil finish. The bluing was perfect, and the bolt polished. It was a very fine piece, and it was deadly. The last fact was a real comfort to Wade's way of thinking that morning. Shelton wished him well, and Wade departed for the rifle range to get familiar with his new-found friend.

Chapter 7

The local TV station sent a reporter and cameraman to check out the story of a missing person. The lag in the reporting was mainly due to the closed mouth of the sheriff and of Wade Larson. Consequently, the news report would be four days old by the time it aired on the evening news from Kalispell. The reporter was incensed at the delay and let the desk sergeant know just how she felt.

"I would like you to know that, in a free society, it is of utmost importance to allow the news media free and unfettered access to any and all breaking news. The public demands information, especially when it is of such dire circumstances. Missing people deserve every break they can get to be found. The sheriff, by withholding vital information like this, is doing, at the very minimum, a gross disservice to the community and possibly is committing obstruction of justice by his actions."

"I'll let the sheriff know your opinion, Miss. But until he finishes his business in the south county, he will not be granting any interviews with the media. I have my instructions. Kindly let yourself out the front door, and feel free to go on to the crime scene to record your video for tonight's TV news."

With that obvious dig and send-off, Jennifer Roslin Beale spun on her heel and fled the confines of the foyer of the Sheriff's Office. She'd show the smart asses in this jerkwater, backwoods of a town that they would pay dearly for snubbing the all-important function of the news media.

Her opinion of her job was just slightly less than her elevated opinion of herself. She was determined to get the story, even if she had to invent it. Lack of facts had never stopped her or her colleagues in the past. Who the hell cared for facts anyway. The news had little to do with fact, but much to do with perception and emotion. Jennifer would get the attention she deserved, one way or another. And she would get the story out to the public, with a healthy dose of her opinion on the whole matter. She was absolutely certain of that fact. If the damned thing that was snatching people would just grab a few more, well then, she would end up being a star reporter and certainly would be in line for an anchor position. Now that was worth the hassle dealing with these fool country bumpkins and the smart-ass sheriff and his rockheaded deputy. She needed some footage, and she had to have it tonight, before the late news hit the screen.

The desk sergeant called Jefferson McDougal on the cell phone. It wouldn't pay to trust that the reporter wasn't listening in on the radio.

"Sheriff, it's a good thing that you aren't here right now. That little, snippy wench, Jennifer Beale, just stormed out of here crying about obstruction of justice, among other things. She got her hair twisted into a knot about the fact that you were not here to listen to her rant and rave about the first amendment and all manner of bullshit about the rights of the people to know, etc. etc."

"Thanks a lot for running interference for me, Bob. I know how you hate the media, which is just about one or two steps below how I hate it. I won't be back until late, just to make sure I don't run into her. Why don't you leave early and get a nice steak on me? I'll see you in the morning."

"Sure enough, boss, and thanks for the steak. I'm packing up right now. Have a good night."

When Jennifer Beale got to the "crime scene", there was next to nothing to see. The construction trailer was still sitting there, but no trucks were parked in front of it. And there were no people around it. There was little to build a story on but for the mystery of another disappearance, without any clues left to lead somewhere.

"Ronnie, lets head for that greasy spoon café out on the old road. I know for a fact that it is the gathering place for the locals around here. There is bound to be someone to talk to over there. This crime scene is as dead as the guy that used to be superintendent here."

Jennifer Beale and Ronnie squeezed into the sub-SUV and skidded around on the wet dirt before getting pointed down the mountain, headed for the "Country Café".

Jennifer was complaining to Ronnie, again, about the lousy cheapskates that ran the TV station. The compact SUV was barely big enough for one person and a small dog, let alone two people. Then there was the camera equipment, Jennifer's travel bag, make-up kit, and her old-fashioned Oscar cooler that held her vitamin water, veggies, dark chocolate, and an ice pack.

"What the hell, Jennifer! Why don't you just knock it off? Every time we hit the field, it is the same old bitchy complaints. Get over it. The station isn't going to buy you a Tahoe. Grow up already; you're past thirty. Things aren't going to get any better any time soon. I don't like the lack of room either, but at least we are not having to drive our own cars on these assignments."

"Ronnie, you can't call me names like that. I won't stand for it. I deserve some respect from you."

"You'll get some respect when you quit whining and get on with the job. How far to the café? I'm getting really hungry.

Chapter 8

It had been over two weeks since the superintendent had disappeared, and no progress had been made on what had happened to him, and more importantly about what had caused his disappearance. The construction company had hired another man to run the job. The work crew had reassembled and were making progress. The heavy rain had stopped, and the country was only treated to an occasional evening or morning shower. The new roadbed was being pushed across the flank of the mountain as fast as the tree fallers could get the forest cut out for the right-of-way. The D-9 and track hoes were making quick work of the stumps. After the fitful start, the company was finally pleased with the progress.

No one else had disappeared, as far as anyone knew, and the fear and panic had subsided to a nuisance level of apprehension. The road crew were, once again, morning and evening customers at the Country Café. Janey Smalley was trying to deal with her terror about the missing and of the beast that had taken seven people so far. Her fear was not unreasonable and was probably a much more realistic acceptance of the situation than what many had adopted. Plenty of beer, loud music, and close association with as many people as possible all combined to push the terror back to a manageable level. The problem with ignoring the strange events of the missing was that the thin veneer of normalcy was not real. It would not sustain any of the locals or the visitors when it all happened again. Then the reality of radical measures would become necessary.

The sheriff understood the reason people were putting a happy face on a bad situation. But he knew it was a brittle facade. He and Wade had discussed it all at length. They were as afraid of its happening again, as was Janey. But being the first ones to have to accept responsibility for any response to another incident caused them to adopt a fatalistic mind set. McDougal and Larson knew for a fact that there were going to be more deaths and disappearances. Whatever the hell the beast was, it was becoming more used to taking people. The deer and elk herds had radically diminished over the last decade. That left few choices for large predators.

Then, the news that everyone dreaded hit them like a freight train. A distant neighbor had stopped by Willie von Vorhees's place to see about buying a hound. What he found sent a chill through his body immediately. There was no answer from the cabin when he knocked, but the door swung open easily. Old dishes crowded the sink, growing mold on leftover food. The propane lights were still burning, making it obvious that Willie had never shut them down. The neighbor heard pitiful wails from the kennel and walked over to see the dogs. On his way, he tripped over a broken Coleman Lantern lying in the thick grass. The dogs sent up a pitiful howling when he came into view. They were emaciated and obviously dying of thirst. He got two plastic buckets, filled them at the hand pump well, and hauled the water to the poor animals. They lapped it up and wanted more. He refilled all of their water dishes and looked around for dog food. It turned out that Willie had a metal bin filled with dry food on the front porch of the cabin. The neighbor got the animals fed as quickly as possible. But he didn't let them out for fear they would run off and be gone for good. Those immediate chores completed, he crossed the yard back to his pickup and grabbed his cell phone. After trying 911 several times and not getting through, he decided to drive around the mountain to where he knew he could get a signal.

The dispatcher came on after a short wait and asked for his information. He explained the situation and told her where he was and that he would wait for word from the Sheriff's Office before heading back to his own cabin.

"Wade, let's get ourselves on over to Willie's place pronto. I want to search the area before any other locals show up and inadvertently destroy evidence. I'm pretty certain he's been taken, too, like the others. Of all people, old Willie should have been keenly aware of what we all know to be some kind of large predatory animal. This thing is like nothing we've dealt with before. I think Willie may have gotten careless, being on his own grounds with his hounds. Something drew him out of the house, and he was exposed to danger. He should have been prepared for the very thing that happened to the road crew superintendent. From here on I want every deputy to carry heavy weapons. And, we are going to warn the populace against any unnecessary travel, entering the woods or any remote area for any reason. I believe that we can rightly figure that we are now under siege."

The news traveled fast, as bad news always does. Like it had been pre-planned, everyone aware of the new situation headed for the café. It was the only meeting place for dozens of miles in any direction. When McDougal and Larson drove into the parking lot, it was already crowded with cars and pickup trucks. The din of conversation washed over them when they stepped inside. The place was literally packed. A hush fell on all when they saw the sheriff and deputy enter the room.

The sheriff didn't waste any time taking charge of the situation.

"Folks, as you have apparently heard, Willie Von Vorhees has gone missing. Wade and I have just returned from Willie's place. We found a broken Coleman lantern about half way to the hound kennels, lying in the grass. There were no animal tracks, save for a few deer prints and, of course, dog tracks. I would appreciate it if someone would go out to his place and get the dogs off to a kennel in Libby. They were starving and are going to need attention. Whoever volunteers for that duty, I want you to get going right away. We are going to enforce a curfew from sundown to sunup until this matter is settled. No one is allowed into the forest until we can eliminate the threat. When you do move around, you should seek out other people to travel with. Every one of you should go armed with heavy weapons, if you have them. Do not venture out of your house at night, no matter what you hear outside. Whatever we have on the loose is big, smart, and deadly. It seems that it is beginning to key in on people as a food source. This is not a time to be careless, people. We are under siege from something that we have not identified, so I warn you to take this seriously. Now is no time to go your own way. Band together for safety. My office is going to patrol all of the roads in this section of the country, with two deputies in each car. It is too dangerous for them to go it alone. Let this be your first and last warning."

The new road crew foreman spoke up for the first time.

"Sheriff, my company has a contract to fulfill, and I intend to do just that. We cannot afford to pull off the job, especially now that we have finally made some progress on the road. I think that you should make an exception for our situation and that we should be allowed to continue with the building."

"I understand your concern about your company and its contract with the state. But no one is going to violate my orders. From now on, there is a curfew from five in the evening to seven in the morning and a full restriction on off-road travel. Not one on your crew is allowed to set foot into the forest. I am officially declaring a state of emergency right this moment. Anyone breaking my order will be arrested and jailed. No contract or loss of revenue will justify the loss of any other person. Your company has already lost one of its most valued employees. It is my job to see that it loses no more.

This discussion needs to shift to the immediate practical concern for the safety of all in this county. If any of those here want to offer constructive advice or help, please stick around. The rest of you need to head off to your places and wait it out, until the threat is eliminated. Be sure to not go alone and to gather with others in your dwellings. We are basically in a state of war and a state of siege."

The order was officially typed and sent out to all departments of the state, the media, the schools, and public places. The sheriff requested manpower help from other jurisdictions, the Sheriff Reserve, and any group of citizens willing to be deputized, in order to patrol the northwest section of the county. He formally requested that the governor mobilize the National Guard. The hunt was on for the monsters terrorizing Lincoln County.

Chapter 9

Jennifer Beale was incensed. Her story had been given over to a senior reporter that the network was sending out from Seattle.

Of all of the damned breaks, this was the worst. Just when she had thought to break into the big time with an exclusive, the network blindsided her in favor of some gold-plated bitch from friggin' Seattle, Washington.

She was ranting to Ronnie about the stab in the back—the unfair, traitorous treatment that she had been subjected to.

"Damn it, Jennifer, I hate to listen to your raving about what's right and wrong. You could care less about what is right, and I know it. This is a perfect example of why you will never make it to anchor. The station and the network are the bosses. The fact that you have let both of them know just how you feel will destroy your potential chances for advancement. The powers that be want the semi-famous haircut from Seattle to handle this one, and you should have kept your mouth shut. Now I may lose my job just because I'm associated with you. You never seem to learn. Maybe you should give some thought about the people that were taken, instead of how you can turn the tragedy into advancement for your own petty ego."

"You can go to hell, as far as I am concerned, Ronnie. You have never appreciated what it takes to do my job. I deserve better from you and from this company, and if that doesn't come my way, well, I am sure that I can do something about that."

"Yeah, you can quit, or get fired, or just do your job, like a good girl."

"Screw you, Ronnie. I won't have you on my team a moment longer. I'll get this story if it kills me. And I aim to cut out that fake-haired bitch from Seattle as fast as possible. The world hasn't heard the last of Jennifer Roslin Beale, not by a damned sight."

"You go off on your own like that, we just may well have heard the very last of Jennifer Roslin Beale. The beast seems to have a penchant for taking solo operators fooling around these woods. I'll be glad to sit this one out, because I am not venturing out into the forest with you, Jenny. Have a nice day for the rest of your life."

Jennifer slammed the door and stiff-legged walked back into her cubicle. She immediately sent off inquires to any and all the news outlets that she could conjure up. There had to be a place for her somewhere, and she was going to find it and claw her way to the top. She believed that she was extremely under-appreciated in her present position. A real change was needed. Just when she should have had a meteoric rise to the top, she got blindsided by some old farts that thought they knew how the news should go. Well, the hell with all of them. She would find a way. Hadn't she always done so. Maybe some other outlet could be convinced to let her run with her story. Then splash it across all of the television news affiliates as an exclusive from someone that really did know the territory and her way around this monster stuff. Just maybe. She would test the water right away.

Coleen "Queen" Quigley waltzed into the Kalispell television station like a conquering hero. All eyes focused on her while she posed in the foyer like she was doing a photo shoot for a slick women's magazine. She wore a black, tight, knee-length skirt with a deep red, low-cut blouse and spike heels with silver straps. Everything about her exuded sex and professional aloofness. Two of the staff members tripped over each other trying to see if they could help her with something, anything at all. She ignored them all, obviously waiting for someone who knew what the hell was going on. She didn't have long to wait. The station manager, Ben Swanson, hurried to her aid like a teenager on his first date. "The Queen" was used to deference, and she condescended a slight smile upon Ben.

"Mr. Swanson, I will be checking into a hotel, and then I will be back here in an hour to set up shop and get to work. If you would be so kind to have someone see that my things are immediately brought to my office. Thank you."

She waited for the "servants" to get her gear out of the cab and placed in an office, then entered her "chariot" for the dash to the "palace". The "hired help" was miffed to the extreme by her behavior and by the fawning and booth-licking by the station manager. "The Big Time" had arrived in Po-dunk--"fly over country". And the locals were "restless" to the extreme.

Something else was restless, too. The two beasts were on the prowl for red meat. Darkness was almost complete, when they found what they were looking for at a small lake, deep within the spruce forest. A cow elk was having a drink, its head down, lapping up water, before heading off to bed down. It never had a chance. Both predators snapped at it at once. It was fairly ripped in two by four huge fangs that cut through muscle and bone like meat cleavers. The beasts feasted on hot, quivering flesh for over an hour before leaving the kill, moving into the wind, then ascending the mountain to a lair. They liked to lie up on ridges and high points, where they could gaze down upon prey. Their hunger satisfied for the time being, the animals dozed off to sleep with full bellies and no cares in their world. Working as a team had resulted in sure kills, especially since they were so very stealthy in relation to their size.

They were almost a perfect match, size for size. At thirteen feet long, some six and a half feet high at the shoulder, and weighing in at almost fourteen hundred pounds, there was nothing in North America that could challenge them for quickness, size, ferocity, and sheer power. Not even the vaunted Kodiak Bear would try a contest against such a beast. They were the ultimate killing machine. Sixteen-inch long fangs, extended from a huge, broad head. Fangs that could plunge into the vitals of any other animal with ease were matched with massively-muscled forearms, giant forepaws, sporting meat hook-like retractable claws that ripped and held their prey. These were meshed to massive back muscles. Their eyes were perfectly adapted to the dark, in which they loved to hunt. They were extremely fast, having great endurance and superior stealth. The beasts were careful not to show themselves to humans. They seemed to know that humans were only dangerous in groups. But otherwise that they very vulnerable and almost stupid when alone. Both animals were practically jet black, except for some mottled brown markings along their flanks. The brown spots actually helped to camouflage them even further, when walking through the forest in daylight.

Paleontologists, as a profession, considered them a prehistoric, defunct species. Almost all scientists believed the kind of animal that the beast represented, had died out at the end of the Pleistocene. Evolutionists' theories had absolutely no room for an animal that was the spitting image of the great "Ice Age" Saber-toothed Cats. It could not be alive and well, walking through the forests of North America. None of the know-it-all scientists would ever believe that such an animal had actually existed for several thousand years, right under the noses of a community of experts such as themselves.

And in the twenty-first century, most all museums, slick magazines, and pretty much all university professors of Paleontology would insist that such animals were extinct. "They" just knew too much about it all to believe anything else. They were certain that they were right, and so, naturally, "they were". In their belief system, it followed that current wisdom should never be subjected to any real serious inquiry. Their minds were closed on the subject. That was a handy feature to promote certainty in any topic. Something could only be if it fit "current wisdom".

The public's blind trust in experts tended to a public ignorance of the fallibility of scientists generally, and geologists and paleontologists in particular. "Just how stories" filled their publications, their museum displays, their textbooks, and their movies. It was all so neat and tidy.

Well, the bloody killing machines up on the high mountain ridge, sleeping with full bellies, were about to shake up the experts' nice and tidy world. If the public ever got a hint of the deception that had been run on them by "experts", heads would roll. Because of the closed system of universities and colleges, that passed on the "current wisdom" as education, there was very little chance that anything would ever really change. Unless and until something out of the supposed dim past walked into the living room and took the wife off the couch and out the door.

Their sacred theories had to be protected and kept from the ranting of "unbelievers" at all costs, even if the theories were wrong. Whenever evolutionary theory was faced with actual evidence that refuted it, right back to its inception, war was declared, and closed minds banded together for protection from the scourge of outside empirical evidence. Philosophy, and recently mysticism, ruled supreme in evolutionary thinking and always had.

But grim reality was about to jump right into the middle of accepted dogma and make a mess of the false norm. Truth and reality sometimes earned a bad reputation by overturning gold-plated opinion, anchored upon the altar of peer review by tenured experts.

Chapter 10

Wade Larson had spent enough time with the
.458 Winchester recoiling against his shoulder
to amass a black, blue, and yellow bruise the
size of a cantaloupe. He was bound to be sore
for a few days, until it healed enough for him
to try it again. He had gotten a decent enough
grouping to feel secure with the piece. And he
was confident that he could hit the thing in its
vitals, if, and it was a big if, he could control his
fear. The thing, whatever it was, had him
spooked more than a little bit. It was beyond
creepy--it was terrifying. And Wade was
terrified, and he knew it only too well. He
wasn't the only one that felt that way, but, so
far, he was the only damned fool that outright,
verbally committed to hunting the beast down
and killing it.

The fact that no one else, including the sheriff,
had volunteered such an opinion did not make
Wade feel any too good. He might have been a

fool to say what he did, but he believed that he must find the animal and put a stop to its killing. But, fool or not, he was not going to tackle the thing alone. He would wait until he had at least one other person committed to the hunt before venturing out into the forest. Whatever it was, it was obviously wary, smart, and stealthy. This was a dangerous game hunt, without an experienced professional acting as a guide and a backup when the moment of truth arrived. He was pitting himself against an apex predator that had destroyed anyone who had had the misfortune to meet it in those lonely, dank woods.

Wade had been reading natural history books, books on North American big game, South American big game, and even African big game. Nothing had stood out as a possibility in his mind. He already knew most of the extant animals described in the several publications. He had even read four or five articles on Big Foot. Those did not satisfy him either. He was at a real impasse to identify the beast. He decided to head to his girlfriend's place to have dinner and discuss the problem with her. She had a college degree in zoology. Maybe Mandy would have an idea.

On the way to her place he picked up a couple of burgers with fries and a six pack of Bud. Nothing like a burger and beer to mull over a problem with. It turned out that it was Mandy's favorite meal, too.

"Hi, Babe, dinner is served."

Wade opened the sack, pulled out the burgers, popped two beers, and they dove into their feast. After dinner, they retired to the couch with two more Buds and began to throw ideas around. Mandy got up and started some popcorn. Wade could not come up with anything that resembled an idea about the creatures that had wreaked havoc upon the little communities of the great northwest mountains and forest.

"Wade, I have wondered about this thing since that day we rode with the posse. It should have left some sign somewhere. It must be something that has paws, paws without extended claws. So it couldn't be a bear, especially a grizzly. It couldn't be a wolf or a dog either. That leaves a cat. Cats, as you know, have retractable claws. And big cats have big feet for their size, feet that spread their weight out. So a big cat with extra-large feet would not necessarily leave tracks in the pine duff that covers most of the forest floor. A cat makes sense, too, because they like the woods more than the open meadows and parks. And they definitely prefer to hunt at night and to lay up in the daytime."

"You're right Mandy. A cat makes sense with what little we know of this beast. A big cat could have taken these people, but it would have to be a very big cat. Mountain lions usually only eat until they are filled, then cover their kill with dirt and sticks so that they can return to feed later. We have never found any kills, left overs, or bodies covered up or otherwise. The person is just gone, completely. Now if this thing was a giant leopard, it could easily drag off its kill and hang it in a tree. But we don't have any giant leopards in the North America. And, besides, no bodies have ever been found in trees, as far as I know. And I have studied every bit of information available about these missing persons, since the first one disappeared. I can think of it as a cat, but it would have to be a cat like we have never seen or heard of. It certainly has to be far larger than an ordinary mountain lion. Another problem that I see is the length of time that these disappearances span. As far as I know, most cats in the wild begin to lose their prowess after a few years. This thing has been around over fifteen years and evidently is as strong as when it started its reign of terror."

"Wade, maybe we are going off on a tangent here. I don't know, but I think that you should look in some other direction. This is way out of the ordinary, for sure. I think we have got to expand our thinking here. But for right now, why don't you open those other beers and come over here, close to me? A little closer contact seems to be the answer for tonight's problem. I'm ready to change the subject to a more intimate discussion. Maybe you could whisper in my ear some of your other ideas. What do you think?"

"I think that I'm done thinking for now."

Chapter 11

Another week had passed since the sheriff had declared a state of emergency. A few locals and one well-known Kalispell reporter had gone off into the woods, in spite of the sheriff's declaration. All three offenders were promptly arrested and spent three days and two nights in jail. On Monday, they bailed out and got their attorneys lined up for the upcoming trials that their offences would lead to.

To say that Jennifer Beale was incensed would be a poor description of the whinny rage she had displayed, when cuffed and ushered into a cell. Having to wait until Monday to see the judge and make bail was, in her mind, the illegal usurpation of all of her rights and an assault upon her person, akin to being led to the gallows. No one in the jail or, for that matter, in the Sheriff's Office gave a damn about what she thought. They had all heard it before, and more. What maddened Jennifer the most was that no one paid the least amount of attention to her. That really rankled. She would sue the county, the sheriff, the commissioners, the state, and the governor if she didn't get satisfaction. She kept telling herself that, while she sat on the miserable cot and endured the stink and close-quarters' association with a couple of doper women that she was locked in with.

Her life was in shambles. She had been replaced by a plastic witch from Seattle, her story had been ripped out of her hands by management, and her long-time cameraman had told Ben Swanson that he wanted to work with another reporter, any other reporter, in fact. Ben, who had always been so nice to her, had suddenly turned mean and nasty and very abrupt concerning "Queen Quigley".

Jennifer wanted to cry, but she was determined not to do it in her present company. That could be saved for later. For now, she impatiently waited for her lawyer to arrive.

Most of the locals and the road crew were making the Country Café their regular stop, morning and evening. Darkness had, once again, settled down upon the little outpost restaurant, and it began filling up with patrons. The juke box was stuffed with quarters, and it played continuously while more people filed in the door.

Janey was extra busy with the evening rush. The business had been surprisingly good, since the curfew and the restrictions on entering the forest had been emplaced. She liked the boisterous company that the added business provided. The girls waiting tables were raking it in, and they were very happy. It seemed to many that the reason for the curfew and closures had been forgotten or pushed back in their minds far enough that it had almost become irrelevant.

But Janey Smalley had not forgotten, nor had she become complacent nor careless. She was still terrified, but she hid it well. She just knew in her heart that the thing was out there, stalking another victim or, probably, multiple victims. Whatever the hell was out there, it had taken up a residence in Janey's mind and heart. She understood that the only way she was going to be freed from the terror was by the death of the damned thing or by her own. It obsessed her night and day, but the nights were the worst. It could be right outside her place, waiting for more bloody meat, right this minute, as far as she knew. There seemed no way that anyone could do anything about the beast. It was a true monster in her mind. She had been drinking more, much more, than usual. And it wasn't beer that she had been draining down her throat. Vodka and more vodka were her choice to numb the terror. It worked until the very early morning, when she had to rise and prepare for the morning breakfasts. Then the hangover and the pain held her in a vice grip. She knew that she had to quit the alcohol, or she wouldn't be able to continue cooking morning, noon, and night. But, for the time being, it had become her only solace.

Obsession was running rampant within many minds concerning the beast. The county seemed to be holding its collective breath, ready to recoil from yet another mysterious assault. It had actually become a state of siege.

Wade Larson was convinced that he had a destiny to fulfill. He had to kill it, period. How that was to happen was beyond him at the present. But he was mysteriously drawn to a final confrontation with the animal.

Jennifer Beale was absolutely certain that her future lay with reporting the story and its eventual outcome. But how she was going to wrest permission to cover the mystery was beyond her, now that the fake interloper from Seattle had been given the go-ahead.

Sheriff Jefferson McDougal had a bad premonition about any confrontation with the beast. He was in no hurry to challenge it. Wade could do whatever the hell he wanted about the friggin' monster, but he did not want any part of hunting the damned thing to ground.

Colleen Quigley considered the whole affair some sort of Po-dunk, trumped-up, horror story, without any real proof that a monster even existed. But she was more than happy to play out the game, in the hopes that she gained even more fame and notoriety in her career. As far as the pouty, little bitch from Kalispell, well, she could go to hell. Colleen had this thing in her hands now, and she wasn't about to relinquish it to a want-to-be fool from such a "loser place like northwestern Montana."

Ronnie had been assigned to help out with Colleen's investigation and, frankly, was more than glad to get away from Jennifer. Oh, Colleen was a complete pain in the ass, sure, but she didn't whine like Jennifer did. No, she just gave orders, expected results, and ignored everyone that she considered unimportant. That, of course, was pretty much everyone except for herself. But Ronnie could work with her, as long as he kept his mouth shut and just did his job. At the present, there really wasn't much to do. No other people had been taken since old man Vorhees. Colleen had voiced her opinion that they needed another missing person, and very damned quick, to get some traction with the story.

The road crew had one thing in mind, and that was a paycheck. Things had been going fairly well since the new super had arrived, until "the block-headed sheriff" had imposed his restrictions. If something didn't break really soon, most of the crew would be forced to look elsewhere for work.

Chapter 12

The wet spring had given way to a wet, early summer. The woods remained soaked, and any venture into them would immediately bring wet clothes and boots. It was damp and cold. The low hanging clouds hung around the peaks and down the lower slopes in scattered clusters of white against the green of the forest.

The beasts were enjoying the results of the wet forest floor whenever they ventured forth from one of their lairs, high upon a ridge. It was easy to sneak up on elk and deer when the conditions were like they were. Their scent tended to hold to the ground; they made no noise while they slunk along, ready to pounce.

It had been two full days since they had killed the last cow elk, and hunger had motivated them to move to a new location. They had waited until night fall to begin seeking out new hunting territory. Down off the spine of a rocky and barren ridge, both beasts casually walked toward a small lake that was surrounded by forest. It looked like a perfect place to ambush their prey.

They stopped suddenly when they heard voices coming from the lake. Going into a full stealthy slink, they moved like a gruesome set of shadows closer to the sounds. What they saw made little sense to them, but they both licked their lips in anticipation of full bellies. There was prey here, and that was all they needed to make their moves to catch it.

A young couple were in the process of peeling off their clothes, getting ready for some skinny dipping. The girl was the first one in the water, quickly followed by her boyfriend. They swam around awhile, then climbed out and toweled off as fast as possible. The two quickly made their way to their tent, where they fell onto air mattresses and began to toy with each other. They were soon into a hot love-making session that neither one of them wanted to rush. Suddenly, they heard something just outside of their tent. They quickly stopped their fun and listened intently to an unearthly rumble and growl. Neither had ever heard such a sound, even in a horror movie. They were sharply aware of huge bodies moving just on the other side of the nylon of the tent. Both of them were too terrified to even scream. They were frozen together.

One of the beasts suddenly lunged forward and ripped the tent fabric to shreds with its massive fangs. Below him lay the entwined bodies of the two lovers. Their eyes wide with fright and uncomprehending horror, they never moved a muscle. The beast opened his mouth and closed it over the man's head like a massive vice. The man was jerked upright, breaking his neck in the process. The woman began to let out one unholy screech and wail after another, until the second monster leaped across the clearing and snatched her off the ground with his massive jaws. She screamed even louder as her body twisted and jerked, until the animal bit all the way down, neatly cutting her in two.

The two beasts fed lazily upon the remains of the dead lovers, before moving off to a distant ridge to lay up and casually lick their fur clean of any remains of the skinny-dipping campers. One great beast took up vigilance on a flat rock that jutted out into space, giving the animal a commanding view of the surrounding country-side. The rising thermals wafted scent upwards to the lookout. Both cats settled into a long, daytime nap.

Wade Larson was on patrol with another deputy, a woman named Suzie Campbell. She had been with the Sheriff's Office for two years and had proved to be a sober, no-nonsense law enforcement professional. Larson was comfortable with her abilities and judgment.

They had just turned off onto a well-used forest road that led to a small lake popular with campers. The lake was about ten miles from the Vorhees property, but Wade knew that if it was a big cat, ten miles was nothing for it to travel on a hunting circuit. Susie and Wade had been checking all camp sites and roads within the area, making sure that the restrictions were being followed.

Upon arriving at the lake, the first thing that they saw was an out-of-state vehicle parked next to the remains of a green nylon tent. Susie drew her Glock .40, and Wade reached around to the rifle rack, grabbed the .458 Winchester, and bolted a round. None of this looked good to the two deputies. Something was very wrong about the scene before them. The tent was ripped, almost like it had been cut, right in two. Both sleeping bags were opened and spread out like blankets. Flies were buzzing around the site in great numbers.

Wade felt the hair on his neck prickle and a shiver went right up his spine. He could smell it--blood. Upon closer examination, it turned out that one of the bags was covered in blood and what looked like intestines. When he turned the bag over, the smell of death was overwhelming.

"Wade, look over to your right. What is that? Is that what I think it is? If it is, I'm going to be sick."

Wade stared at something at the edge of the clearing, and the something stared back with sightless eyes. A human head was lying alone at the far side of the campsite. He walked over to it and saw that it was a man's head that had been neatly severed from its body.

"Susie, we've got solid evidence that something killed a person here. Go back to the vehicle and get our camera. I am going to stand here with this elephant rifle, in case whatever the hell is out there decides to return. The animal could be close, laying up after eating its fill."

"Yeah, Wade, you keep that elephant gun handy; I've had a bad feeling about this whole thing ever since that construction foreman got taken."

Wade took twenty-five pictures of the scene, the head, and the tent and bags. Susie walked down to the lake to look at some items near the water's edge. It turned out to be the couple's clothes. Now they had more evidence. And they were aware that there were at least two people missing. It was pretty obvious to both deputies that a couple had gone swimming and then gone back to the tent, leaving their clothes in a pile at the water's edge.

"What a hell of a thing to think about, Wade. These two were probably screwing each other when they were attacked and killed. They were obviously skinny-dipping in the lake before they went to the tent. I found towels with the clothes over there. So we have two bodies missing and probably eaten by this time. But how did it get both of them so easily? And there is no evidence that I can see that the people were eaten here, where the killing took place."

"Susie, go back to the truck and pull my .300 magnum out of the rack. It's loaded, but you'll need to bolt a shell into the chamber. I am beginning to think that there must be two of these bastards running around in these woods."

Wade began a serious search for tracks in the damp ground. He had noticed some smudge-like shallow depressions when he was scanning the campsite initially. Walking around the clearing, he came upon a print, actually several prints, now that he looked harder. But it was a print like no print he had ever seen in all of the years he had lived in the area. It was friggin' huge. The thing was about sixteen inches across. Faint pad marks without any claw prints indicated a cat. But what a cat! No big mountain lion had feet like this thing had. Wade became certain, the more he stared at the print, that, whatever it was, it was a monstrosity. He suddenly realized that he was not over-gunned with the .458. If anything, he might want something bigger. What a hell of a beast was loose out there!

Wade called the office on his cell phone and got ahold of the sheriff.

"Sheriff, I've got an incident scene out at Little Mirror Lake that you need to see. We have our first real evidence of a killing, most likely two killings, and evidence of what it might be that has been terrorizing the neighborhood. Bring your evidence kit and body bag. Susie and I are examining the site right now for more evidence. And, Sheriff, please don't let the damned news media get wind of this. Better bring some food along, because it will be a long day out here, I'm sure."

Wade went back to the tracks and began taking pictures from all angles. He found other prints across the clearing leading into the forest from a different direction than the first set. Two, for sure, was his immediate conclusion. He realized that the situation was tremendously compounded by the fact that there were at least two of the animals in the vicinity. It would be more than doubly dangerous to hunt them to ground. Two monstrous, killing machines, working together was beyond dangerous--it was more likely suicidal.

Chapter 13

Colleen Quigley had been chomping at the bit for days. There had been no new missing persons, and the blasted rain was worse than Seattle, with nothing to see other than more trees. She had gotten surly and mean and had even less tolerance than usual for fools and idiots. The fact that that dumb bunny, Jennifer Beale, was a combination of both pleased Colleen and angered her at the same time. The stupid wench was still whining to management about her lost story, like it was a lost puppy dog or something. Colleen was determined to stick here in this "fly over country", as long as it took to keep Jennifer from taking over the story. So far, Colleen had seen nothing but fear and ignorance from these morons around town. A few rednecks had bragged that they could hunt the monster down, given the right incentive, but they had gathered no benefactors so far and were obviously never going to get any. More bullshit and hot air, just like all of the other fools that this country seemed to spawn.

Ronnie had proved to be an exception to the local loons that populated the area. He kept to himself, provided good coverage and video when he was told to, and seemed to have no love for Jennifer Beale. He had also told Colleen that he would keep a diligent watch over the Sheriff's Office, it's radio traffic, and any obvious emergency movements that may occur. He had a police scanner that he kept on continuously. So it was that Ronnie picked up some chatter about an incident scene out at Little Mirror Lake. There were several deputies heading out there fast. Ronnie figured that it could be the break they had waited for, so he called Colleen immediately. They were on their way to the lake in ten minutes, going as fast as the little compact SUV would go.

Colleen put up with the cheap little car, kept her thoughts to herself, and trusted that she had finally gotten a break in the story. Time would tell, but all of the chatter, speeding cop cars, and the obvious excitement in their voices gave hope to the "Queen" of the reporters. She touched up her face, combed her blond hair into an even higher peak, and took a long drink of a Starbucks mocha.

Ronnie followed a sheriff's pickup around the last bend before the lake turn off and saw it dart to the left onto the narrow gravel lane that led to Little Mirror Lake. He followed close behind. When they arrived, there were three other sheriff's vehicles parked next to each other, with their red and blue lights flashing.

"Ronnie, get your camera rolling now; I am going to talk to the sheriff right away. Something is definitely wrong, and something that's wrong, some tragedy or emergency, is our bread and butter. Stick close to me, and be sure to avoid taking video of my face from my bad side. Keep me in the picture at all times, no matter what else is in the background. We are going to give the public its first taste of proof that the monster may exist. Now hustle your butt up; here we go."

Wade saw her first and gave out a sharp whistle to warn the sheriff, who had just placed the head in a body bag. McDougal zipped the bag closed and stood, just as Colleen accosted him face to face.

"What has happened here, Sheriff? Have you finally gotten some proof of whatever has been terrorizing this quiet, friendly, sleepy, little area for weeks now? There is a very concerned public out here that deserves to know just what threatens them. They need to know what's been lurking in these dark woods."

Colleen closed her mouth and looked at the sheriff in a very aggressive and accusatory manner. The sheriff was trapped, and he knew it. The camera was rolling, and he was on the spot. He instantly assumed a concerned posture, a sympathetic facial pose, and began to speak like a politician.

"I can tell you that the Lincoln County Sheriff's Office is actively involved in a crime scene investigation. We have another missing person's situation here, and there may be new forensic evidence that might give up some important facts, which heretofore, have not been available from any of the other incident scenes."

"Sheriff, just what are you doing about the safety of the public. It seems that there has been a dangerous slip-up in your current policy, if you now believe that you have more than one missing person."

Colleen had just dug the knife in the sheriff's back, and he knew that any response would draw ridicule from the viewing public. So he did what any law enforcement officer would do--he cited his precautions, the curfew, and the restrictions on entering the forest, especially at night.

"Well, the alleged restrictions haven't worked out so well for these folks from Oregon. It seems obvious that some kind of foul play is involved. It's also obvious that your office seems to be overwhelmed, and unable to control its own jurisdiction."

She hit a nerve with that last blast against the sheriff. His face turned dark, his eyes narrowed down, and he took two steps forward so that his face was the only thing in the camera lens. Then he spoke.

"This is a crime scene. There may be various kinds of evidence scattered around this clearing. Our forensic expert is right now trying to collect as much evidence as possible. As of this minute, civilians are restricted from the site. I am going to clear the area in order to protect any other evidence. You and your cameraman need to back out and get on the highway right now. You may have already contaminated the crime scene. It's time to move out, Ronnie."

Ronnie knew Sheriff McDougal. He knew that there wouldn't be a second warning. He told as much to the "Queen" and began packing up his camera. Colleen was furious at the treatment she had just received. Her very soul was on fire after being ordered out by a bumbling idiot like McDougal. She would show this clown how she dealt with obstinate jerks, like a country bumpkin sheriff. Ronnie caught her eye and shook his head in an emphatic, "No". She caught herself ready to launch into a long string of cussing. Something in Ronnie's face and demeanor told her to hold her tongue and get into the car. She wasn't sure, but Ronnie looked kind of nervous. So, against her supposed better judgment, she relented and allowed Ronnie to drive her away from Little Mirror Lake and down the highway.

"Ronnie, what the hell did I just allow you to do? It is against all of my instincts and better judgment to pull off from that lake. Something big is going on, and that smartass politician of a sheriff isn't going to stymie my efforts to get the news out to the public."

"Colleen, listen to me. The sheriff would have probably run us off anyway, but your verbal slap in his face, when he is right in the middle of a sensitive investigation, one that may finally bring some explanation to all of our unsolved disappearances, was a step too far. Sheriff McDougal is nobody's fool, so don't play him like one. He never gives a second warning when he makes a declaration like the one he just made. You may not be aware of it, but a County Sheriff is the most powerful position in all of state government. It doesn't pay to cross McDougal. He was about ready to arrest us for obstruction of justice. He can make it stick, news people or not. The jail is not someplace I want to cool my heels. We wouldn't be out for days. I've seen him do just that. He has a tight connection with all of the judges in the court house, and they will not look with favor on anyone screwing around a crime scene, especially this one. The people of Lincoln County are spooked by whatever is taking people. Some of those taken were friends or relatives of the very people you were taking pot shots at just now. Deputy Wade Larson lost his nephew just under three years ago. His sister's husband left her because of her on-going grief. Wade is really easy to rouse when it comes to that. So we have to be careful if we want to stay out of the slammer and get the story out. You will need to apologize to the sheriff for your comments, if you want to get access again to any crime scene in this county."

"I'll be damned if I apologize to that egomaniac loon. This isn't the 19th century when the sheriff packed a big .44 and shot anyone who crossed him. McDougal may think he's Wyatt Earp, but I sure as hell don't think so. I aim to get the story, get the footage, and maybe even find this poltergeist that everyone is so scared of. We are going to begin cruising these back roads until you can get some footage of this supposed monster."

"Well, Colleen, I guess I just wasted my time and breath. You don't seem to get it, no matter what the facts are. First thing, right off, I am not going monster-hunting with you or with anybody else, period. Second thing, I do not intend to be arrested and then tried for obstruction of justice, which any idiot right out of law school could prove in five minutes. Third thing, you may not respect the beast that is out there, but I sure enough do. I live here, and I know that these missing people have been taken by something. Driving around in the dark out here will get you killed. Did you happen to notice the remains of the campers' tent? I did. It was ripped in half, and there was blood and something else all over it and all over their sleeping bags. Also, the deputies seemed to congregate over on the far edge of the clearing, staring intently at the ground. I think that they have found the tracks of whatever it is. So here is where we come to an agreement or where we part ways. What do you intend to do?"

"Never in my career have I had a cameraman talk like you just did. I run this show, and I plan to keep running it, with or without your help. I'm sure that I can bring in my own cameraman to do your job, if that is what you want. Otherwise, you need to get your ass in gear, shut your trap, and follow orders. You got it, mister?"

Oh, sure I got it, Colleen. You are the "Queen," and we all are your servants and boys. Well, you know what happens when the queen bee dies don't you? The bee hive feeds royal jelly to another female bee, and, presto, a new queen. Colleen, you can die out here, with or without a story, and another queen will step into your place and get the story out over your dead body. I know that you have no respect for anyone other than yourself, but you just might want to consider how many people have mysteriously died in these woods. And some of them almighty recently. There is some kind of beast roaming this countryside, whether you think so or not. So, no, I am not going to get my "ass in gear", as you so arrogantly put it. I quit right here and right now. Go ahead and get your lackey from Seattle, continue with your superior attitude, and keep running over people. See how it works out here in the sticks. You are bound to get a rude awaking from any further dealings with the sheriff. This might be your last chance to really consider that whatever is out there has absolutely no respect for you. You are a complete, arrogant fool and the most unreasonable bitch that I have ever had the displeasure to meet."

Ronnie put the SUV in gear and stomped on the pedal, spinning the tires and laying a whole six-inch strip of rubber. He drove fast back to Libby, with the local country music station on high volume, avoiding any further conversation with Colleen Quigley.

Ronnie slammed into a parking curb and turned off the little SUV, grabbed his camera equipment, and walked away without a backward look at the car and its incensed, steaming occupant. He threw open the door to the studio and searched out the station manager, Ben Swanson.

"Ben, I need to talk with you right away. I've made a decision, and you should know about it from me first, before Collen Quigley gets in here."

"Hey, Ronnie, what's up? You seem agitated, and that's not like you. You are always my relaxed, low-key guy, when everyone else is overly excited over one thing or another."

"Ben, I just quit the job with Colleen Quigley, and I want nothing to do with that lunatic that our lousy network pawned off on us. She's poison, and she's a train wreck, wrapped with a fake smile and crowned with fake blond hair. She almost got us thrown into the slammer for obstruction. The sheriff is not going to allow her anywhere near the crime scene. On top of that, she is planning to go out in the dark, monster-hunting. I told her that I was not going hunting for the thing and that she might want to consider how many people have recently disappeared after dark, in this neck of the woods. Ben, don't call me for a while. I've got to sort this out, and I don't want to work again until I do.

The frequency of these attacks has picked up dramatically. Anyone going off halfcocked into the forest is liable to end up on the missing persons' list. Listen, Ben, I just saw what was left of two people--a little blood, some other substance smeared on their sleeping bags, a ripped tent, and a lump of some kind zipped up in an otherwise empty body bag. The thing is evidently eating its victims, and that is why no bodies have been discovered. Ben, whatever this thing is, it's feeding on humans. I think that it is time for our community to collectively do something to protect ourselves. Maybe you can talk it around and come up with something. I'm in no mood to do anything right now. I'll call in, in a day or so. Good luck dealing with her highness, the 'Queen'."

Chapter 14

The construction crew had been pulled off the job for the time being and had been assigned to a road project in the eastern part of the state. It was a repair and replace contract that the company had in progress. It wouldn't hurt for the extra crew to join the original one and get the job completed quickly. The bosses did not want to lose the personnel, waiting around for something to change in Lincoln County. So the entire crew was ordered to strike camp and head off toward Glendive, Montana, to work on highway 200.

The loss of seventeen regulars cut down on the profits at the Country Café, but it really didn't hurt Janey's bottom line much. The regular customers were consistent, and she could count on them. Then there was the increased presence of more deputies taking up some of the slack.

Janey was glad that the cops frequented her place. She felt much safer having law enforcement around, now that the animal attacks had increased. Her fear continued to mount, but she was reasonable, too, so she trusted in the fact that none of the attacks had occurred around any population centers. If that was what the café was, then she figured that she was actually safer here than most any other place in this portion of the county.

The juke box played on, loud and comforting to her ears. Some of the locals were singing along with the country lyrics, while she was busy cooking for the dinner hour. The girls were waiting tables, like any other night.

The door opened, and in walked the woman from the Seattle TV station, along with a burly-looking man dressed in slacks and a windbreaker. He wore a Seattle Mariners ball cap and carried a large television camera. They took a seat in the middle of the café and surveyed the room, missing nothing in their perusal of the patrons, who were busily going about the business of eating dinner and talking.

Sally brought the newcomers menus and water and waited for the order. Hamburgers, French fries, and beer were their choices. Janey slapped a couple of patties on the grill and dropped a fry basket of spuds into the hot grease. Sally served a picture of beer and two mugs to the duo at the table.

An hour had gone by since the TV woman had entered the room, and she and the cameraman were still sitting at their table. It was full dark outside. Some of the café windows on the east side of the building looked out into the fringes of the forest, just across the side parking lot, maybe twenty-five feet wide. Usually, no one parked there, unless it was a trailer rig that needed the length. Tonight, the lot was empty, lit by the glow from inside the café. Janey had taken a seat at the counter and was resting up after the evening rush. She had a mug of beer in her hand and had just lifted it up for a drink, when something caught her eye. She was staring at a face, reflected in the stainless-steel refrigerator door, in the bank of cabinets across from the counter. The windows gave off enough light to cause a reflected image on the stainless-steel door, like a mirror. The face was intently staring right at her back. She was overcome by terror and could not move, scream, yell, or even faint. The reflection was of a monster like she could never imagine. It had a huge, broad head that sported long, wide fangs from a mouth that just couldn't be real. The eyes were wide-set and looked yellow-green. It didn't move a muscle, but it held its gaze on her.

Janey finally caught Sally's attention when she spun around and pointed right at it. The result was recognition by Sally of the monster outside, followed by a scream that started low and climbed in intensity to an ear-splitting crescendo. And then another scream climbing to the same crescendo. Sally was pointing at it, too, and most of the customers looked up to see what was causing the ruckus. The creature glided into the darkness before anyone else could get a glimpse of it. Then the noisy rattle of a diesel engine of a semi-truck, pulling into the parking lot, broke the tension in Janey, and she began to yell and scream herself. She rose from her chair and backed away from the counter, covering her mouth with both hands, and began to weep. She realized that she was shaking uncontrollably, talking gibberish, and making no sense at all.

A sudden commotion at the front door ushered in the truck driver and his ride-along girlfriend. They were regulars at the café, once a week, on their run from the coast to stops on the "high line" route across Montana. His name was Jed and hers was Molly. They stopped abruptly after entering, when they looked up at the patrons of the restaurant. The diners showed different degrees of shock and fear, including the strange-looking woman with the fake hair in the middle of the room.

"Just what the hell is going on here, Janey? We've never done anything to scare you or your customers. But if I didn't know better, I would swear that all of you folks are scared silly of me and Molly. I've never seen the like. What's wrong here, people?"

Janey was trying to calm down so she could speak, but her shaking continued. Sally was crying hysterically and couldn't stop. Janey pulled herself together enough to talk.

"I'm sorry, Jed, but no one is accusing you of scaring anybody here. It was just circumstance that you came in right after we had the worst scare of our lives. Sally and I saw the thing, looking in the window at us, that has been killing people in our county. I will try to go on, but I am going to have a drink before I attempt to continue with this. Does anyone else want a drink?"

There was a unanimous answer, so the other waitress, Lenny, helped Janey serve up the drinks. Janey was on her second vodka by the time they had drinks in everyone's hands. Sally gulped down a slug of rum and collapsed on a chair, still crying.

Janey began to explain to the room what she had seen, when she noticed that the cameraman was recording, while the Seattle woman gave him instructions.

"What do you think you are doing, running that camera in my place, without asking my permission?"

"Look, honey, after you and the waitress went bonkers just now, I thought that we needed to record your statement so that you don't change it or get it wrong later. It can't hurt to have an accurate record of what you saw, can it?"

What the "Queen" heard in return was so out of her ordinary experience, where everyone in the city could hardly wait to be on camera, that it shocked her into silence.

"You and that camera man get the hell outa my place of business. I'm calling the cops right now, and you had better be gone by the time I get off the phone, or some of these men here will throw you out on your ear."

"Damn straight, Janey, you tell 'em. We'll handle this situation anyway you like."

Several rough-looking locals stood up and walked over to the "Queen's" table.

Janey was on the phone to the Sheriff's Office, speaking with Wade Larson, requesting him personally to get to her place as fast as possible.

"Look, Janey, hold your ground, and don't say another word to that reporter. Another deputy and I are on our way. See you shortly. By the way, don't let anyone mess around in the side parking lot. There is probably evidence of that thing's presence out there. We need to get a good look. And I hope that you can calm down by the time we arrive. I want to interview you personally. This is very important. Hang on, Janey. Good bye."

Colleen Quigley was damned if she was going anywhere. This was where the action was, and she meant to have it all on tape, whether the restaurant woman liked it or not. She was the news reporter, and this was news that needed exposure. It was the break that she had waited for long enough in this miserable, rat hole corner of the world. No way was she leaving, especially now that the waitress seemed to be calming down. This would be the perfect time to get her eyewitness testimony. Colleen said nothing to Janey. She directed her cameraman to follow her across the room to record the interview.

Janey had just hung up with Deputy Larson when she saw that Colleen had not vacated the premises, but instead was headed for Sally with the cameraman in tow. This was all she needed to call in her cavalry.

"Boys, it looks like the news people don't listen very well. I think it is time that we got some respect around my place. Get them out of here, right now."

Colleen saw the locals make their move and warned her cameraman.

"Doug, you better get ready for something, because the local numbskulls are coming."

Doug was a tough-guy type that looked the part, which was usually enough to scare off most all comers but the really determined ones. Doug had been in a couple of fights and had won easily, so he wasn't concerned about these clowns in this backwater dump. He set the camera down and assumed a defensive position with his hands well up, covering his chin. It looked professional and intimidating. But looks can be deceiving.

The three men walked right up to him and told him to get the hell outa the restaurant. Doug told them to screw themselves. The first to make a move kicked Doug square between the legs. When he dropped his hands, the other two put him in an arm bar and lifted him off his feet, dragging him out the door. Then they swung ponderous fists into each side of Doug's head. He went out cold and fell in a heap. They returned for Colleen, grabbed her by the hair and the arms, and perp-walked her outside, got her keys to the SUV, and tossed her inside. They dragged Doug to the car, grabbed him, threw him into the front seat, and told Colleen to drive. White-faced, she drove off in a hurry. Janey walked over to the camera, picked it up, and stashed it behind the counter. Wade would probably want to look at it.

Chapter 15

The two big cats had run from the sound of the semi-truck pulling into parking lot. They had been right on the verge of attacking the people that they could see within the café. Their natural fear of men in groups had held them back for a couple of minutes, but hunger had won the day, and they would have snatched Janey and Sally, but for the arrival of the noisy truck.

Both beasts moved off uphill, headed for the spine of the ridge that ran at a perpendicular angle to the highway. They saw the SUV pull out of the parking lot and head for town, its lights eventually disappearing into the gloom. The animals were hungry, but still cautious when it came to more than one or two people to stalk. Their natural curiosity had added to their hunger and had overcome their reticence to draw close to groups of men. But for the time being, there was just too much activity for them to hang around the restaurant locale. They moved as one across the ridge and descended toward a creek bottom that held a succession of meadows. It was a perfect place to ambush an elk or a moose.

The darkness was their friend, and they loved to hunt in the night when sharp-eyed prey could mistake their presence for a large boulder or an abrupt ledge. They could hold perfectly still for long minutes before pouncing on an unsuspecting animal.

A cow and calf moose fed along in the marshy ground, right in the middle of a meadow. The cats had noticed them as soon as they had reached the edge of the trees. The wind was right, so that neither moose had any idea than anything dangerous or unusual was nearby. The cats never moved a muscle as the moose came nearer. They instinctively understood that one cat would take the cow and the other the calf. The cow moose got a whiff of cat, just as the monster closed with her from the shadows. The calf never had a clue. One second it was grazing on the meadow, the next it was quivering in its death throes, spiked through by wicked fangs that had severed its spinal cord.

The two beasts settled down about a quarter mile from the lake and began to gorge upon hot, red, moose meat. There would be enough to satisfy their need for a few days. Growling and snarling from time to time, the monsters took their time with the kills. A few birds had landed in the nearby trees, hoping for some scraps to come their way. But they would have to wait until the cats retired to lay up and sleep off their bloody meal. A small pack of coyotes began to circle the moose carcasses, but they dared not venture too close to the cats. More than one of their kind had made a mistake, a final one, and had ended up as coyote dessert.

The Sheriff's Office was a-buzz with reports, calls, and rumors. Most of the patrons of the Country Café had called 911 as soon as they had gotten within cell range. Bob was on duty as Desk Sergeant, fielding the calls as the dispatcher fed them to him.

Wade Larson and the other deputy had arrived at the Country Café. They had just completed a quick search for tracks along the side parking lot. There were tracks deep enough in the damp ground to make good plaster casts from. As soon as the forensic tech arrived, he could finally get a solid set of prints. The animal that had ventured so close to the window had left very good front and back impressions. Wade could not get over the size of the paw prints from the front feet. He measured them at slightly over fifteen inches. Anything that had feet of that size was huge. A cold chill ran up his spine when he considered the monster he intended to hunt down. The thing was beginning to get into his head, and Wade really didn't like the thoughts he was having about the path he had chosen. It was apparent that it would take more than one hunter to bring these two goliath cats down. That he was certain of.

The forensics expert arrived and got to work. That freed Wade up for the interviews with Janey and Sally.

"Janey, I want to start with you. Then I'll speak with Sally before I bring both of you together to try and get a consensus. So, Janey, tell me what happened--everything and anything that you can recall. It doesn't have to be in any kind of order right now; I just need you to relate what you saw.

 And before we get started, would you mind if we got ourselves a couple cups of coffee?"

"Feel free to get anything you would like, Wade, you and the other deputy, or anyone else for that matter. Help yourselves."

Wade and the other deputy, Jack Wilson, poured coffee and grabbed up a couple of bear claws from the counter.

Janey described her experience and her impressions of the animal she had witnessed. She had some trouble continuing her narrative a few times, when she was overcome by a full range of emotions. She was just barely keeping herself together for the sake of the information she knew that the officers wanted so dearly. When she was about done, she suddenly remembered the camera under the eating counter.

"Wade, I just remembered that we have a camera that the news crew was using. I believe there is some video footage of my beginning to describe what I saw. It's right here under the counter."

Wade picked up the camera and pushed "Play". Janey, wild-eyed, was hysterically describing the encounter, when she suddenly, verbally accosted the news people and told them to shut it down. The video ended quickly.

"How did you get this camera, Janey?"

"Well, that snooty wench didn't leave when I ordered her out of my café. I caught her trying to get Sally to tell her side of the story. I asked some of the guys to usher her and the cameraman out the door and off the premises. They took care of the both of them. The cameraman forgot to take his camera with him when he left."

"That, is obviously the shortened version of whatever happened, to run off that "snooty wench". I think that I can fill in the blanks about this little difference of opinion and probably how the two news-people left the property. I would expect that it involved some kind of physical coercion by any number of local talents. Maybe some guys like Lew, Jeff, and probably big Joe. But there is no need to get into any of that at this time. We have two monsters to kill before they can wreak anymore havoc upon our friends, neighbors, or tourists. Minor altercations are bound to occur when there is this much fear and tension rife in the community."

Wade called Sheriff McDougal to apprise him of the developing situation. The sheriff put in a call to the state to request any assistance that they could spare. The trail was hot, and Sheriff McDougal needed more manpower than he had available. He also called the helicopter pilot and put him on standby for first light in the morning.

McDougal understood that he needed bigger weapons in the hands of his officers, if they were going to face these monstrosities. He began thinking about and planning a large operation to bring these beasts to bay. Also, he couldn't shake the grim premonition that was stalking his mind, like one of the big cats themselves. There was a day of reckoning coming--he knew it in his gut. Little butterflies were fluttering in there, and he didn't like feel of it one bit.

Chapter 16

Colleen Quigley returned to the Kalispell TV station in a subdued manner. She had actually been scared for her life, when the three "brutal thugs" had grabbed her by the hair, pinned her arms behind her, and marched her to the car. She was not used to the kind of treatment she had received at the hands of the "creatins" in "that dive of a café". She was incensed by the assault, but her reaction was something new for her. She had begun to think about tossing this assignment and returning to Seattle. There was something too raw and elemental about the place and the people that she could not fathom. Her aggressive bullying tactics had elicited unbending resistance and distain and had resulted in violence against herself and her cameraman. It was something that she had never experienced before. These hick people were really different. They had no respect for the press, and, as far as she was concerned, no respect for women. Colleen was facing a population that gave as rough as they got.

It just wasn't fair in her mind that anyone would contend with a journalist to the point of assaulting her. She was really a coward at heart, and she hid behind the screen of radical feminism. She talked about equality but actually believed none of it. What she believed in was female entitlement, superiority, and deference to that ideal. In Seattle, she could bully anyone that tried to resist her aggressive pushiness. The cover of equality gave her every advantage out there. Here, in the most remedial, backward thinking society that she had ever encountered, she realized no advantage. She was sure that she got just the opposite. The idea of being ordered out of a trashy, little establishment, like Janey's café, burned like fire. She would talk with the network. They could send some other lackey out here. She wanted to pack up and get back to civilization. They could have their supposed monsters. The hell with monsters, both man and beast.

Doug had finally come to when they had pulled into the hotel parking lot. He was bleeding from one ear, his head was swelled to half again its normal size, and he could barely move due to the kick between the legs. He groaned loudly when she set the parking break.

"Doug, can you make it to your room, or should I drop you at the hospital?"

"I can make it. Just don't expect me to be on the job in the morning. I hurt like hell, and I'm going to sit it out tomorrow. I think that you and I bit off a little more than what we bargained for. Maybe we should bag this assignment, Colleen, and get back to Washington."

"If you feel that way, Doug, I'll call the network and see what I can do for you. I'm not certain that I want to leave just yet, but I will wait for the bosses to make that determination. In the meantime, see if you can get into your room. I'll call first thing in the morning."

"OK, Colleen, that sounds good, and thanks for your understanding. See you in the morning."

Wade Larson got home late. He had eaten at Janey's, so he grabbed a beer from the fridge. He had called Mandy on the way into Libby. She knocked and opened the front door at the same time.

"It's really good to see you, Babe, after what I've been through today. This case has just taken a turn. It really isn't for the better, but we are now getting much closer to figuring out what kind of creature is out there. The damned things came right up to the Country Café and looked in the windows. I'm certain that they were going to take Janey and her waitress, Sally, right out of the restaurant in front of twenty other people. If it hadn't been for a semi-truck pulling into the parking lot, those two women would be dead and in the bellies of those monsters. It was that close."

"Oh, Wade, what are we going to do? These things are freaking me out! They are getting more dangerous every day. It is like African lions get when they turn man-eater. They find out how easy it is to pluck one or two people out of a remote location; then they figure that people are scared of them, and they get more and more aggressive. Wade, I don't care how powerful that gun is that you borrowed--you are not going after these things by yourself, period. With two of them, you won't stand a chance."

"You don't seem to have much faith in my ability to shoot when the time comes."

"This has nothing to do with faith and shooting. This is all about two man-eating cats that are like something out of a horror movie."

"Yeah, I know. I think you're right on this, Mandy. I faced up to that fact when I was measuring the size of the front paw print in the mud of the parking lot. Mandy, the thing has feet fifteen inches across. It must weight three quarters of a ton. What the hell kind of cat is that big? A Bengal or Siberian tiger is about six hundred pounds, and they are huge. What is this that's loose in our woods?"

"Wade, I don't know, but it sure isn't anything that is known anywhere in modern times. I've never heard of any cat that size. None of my books, classes, or lectures on fauna of the world mentioned that such monsters still roam the earth."

"You just said something incredibly important. The last part of your sentence was, "monsters still roam the earth." Just what kind of monsters used to roam the earth, Mandy? What if these things are some kind of throwback, or even a beast that hasn't been discovered in modern times? Do you know of any cats of this size in the dim, prehistoric past? I would really like you to think about this. We might be on the verge of figuring this thing out."

"Wade, what did Janey tell you about what she saw?"

"It was very different than what I expected to hear, but after measuring the tracks and thinking about our conversation just now, it makes sense. She said the thing had a massively wide head, with wide set eyes that were a yellow-green. It seemed to be mostly black with some brownish spots. The hair was short, without any mane, like an African lion has. And the almost unbelievable factor was the enormously long canine teeth. She was sure that they were well over a foot long."

Wade, honey, you just described a saber-toothed cat from the Pleistocene era and the end of the Ice Ages. But with one big difference. No saber-toothed cat skeleton has ever been discovered that would support something of the size you are thinking. The largest such cat was discovered in China some years back. The paleontologists and mammalian experts that study forensics associated with animal size believe the Chinese cat was about the average size of a male polar bear, or about a thousand pounds."

"What if they are wrong? Who's to say, since they only have one extra-large example of a saber-toothed cat? What if they were normally extra-large, like this thing in our backyard? There must have been prehistoric factors that led to gigantic animals. I've seen prehistoric buffalo skulls that dwarf anything alive today. Mandy, we live in one of the most rugged and remote places on earth. The forest here is practically uninterrupted for thousands of square miles. What do we actually know about what could be lurking in these woods? We do know that some kind of monster is taking people right under our noses, and now we have eye witnesses as to what the thing looks like."

Chapter 17

There had been very little news, in the last week, from the Yaak country and Lincoln County about whatever had been happening to people who ventured alone into the woods. The general public had about a three-day attention span, and, after that, the ridiculous emotion-driven dribble coming out of the networks turned most people off, or bored them to death. With no new or exciting news about the disappearances in Northwest Montana, most people forgot what the original uproar was all about. They settled back into their boring existence, waiting for the next "big thing" to splash across the nightly news, as it was erroneously called.

So it was that hikers and tourists began nibbling around the edges of the restricted area put off limits by Sheriff McDougal. A wilderness survival group of young adults, from Washington State University, had been planning their trip to Montana for over a year. They felt that they should not be denied access to the Cabinet Wilderness, just because some retard, backward, redneck sheriff was trying to keep people out of the back-country. He had obviously faked-up a story of monsters in the mountains, with the probable intention of keeping activists' groups away from his neck of the woods. It was particularly galling to the dedicated leader of the group. Because he believed that wild lands could only be saved from destruction by active participation, like hiking in to access the most remote parts of the wilderness, which was obviously set aside for people just like them. Since they "felt" that they were uniquely equipped to spread the gospel of the salvation of wilderness, they would later take to social media to document their experience in the Cabinet Wilderness. They just "knew" that they were the "élite of élite", when it came to caring for the environment and, particularly, the wilderness. In their minds they were the heroes of modern-day activism. And, as any activist understands, a dedicated mind was necessary to achieving victory over the forces of darkness--the redneck idiots that wanted to drive four-wheel drive trucks to the tops of the mountains, cut down the forests, and make parking lots of the meadows. There was righteous work to be done, and these elite believers were willing to work, that was for damned sure. Most importantly, they believed, so seven out of the larger group of environmental warriors at school made ready to hit the trail into the heart of the Cabinet's.

With so much to patrol, the Sheriff's Office was hard put to control the access of determined people who insisted on venturing forth into wild country. The sightings of the beasts at Janey's place had concentrated the deputy's search around the area of the café. No one had patrolled down Highway 56 for three days. Therefore, two Subaru station wagons and a lone Prius, parked along the access to the wilderness, were not noted law enforcement. Regulars and tourists ignored the vehicles and proceeded on their own ways. It was what one might call the setting for a perfect storm.

The big cats had made a hasty retreat from the café that night the semi-truck had scared them off. They had killed and fed for several days off of the two moose. And then they had continued south from the last kill, making a large loop as was their regular habit. They, too, liked wilderness country and were enjoying the change of habitat, as they ascended the Cabinet Mountains. Plenty of game inhabited the mountains, and the pickings were always good in the particular region that they had just entered.

The saber-toothed cats had been laying up for the day along a wide ridge, that led off to the highest of the Cabinet peaks. There was a game trail that the elk favored, just below the flat rock that the cats perched on. Darkness would soon envelope the mountains; then the big cats would begin their hunt. Their bellies were practically empty, and they would need to kill soon or begin to feel the effects of the lack of meat.

Daniel Klosterman, Ph.D., in Environmental Land Management, had had his eye on a particular woman that had joined the hiking group about a month before the expedition into the Cabinets. She was young and supple of mind and body, and Klosterman was infatuated with her. In fact, he could not think straight whenever he considered what might occur if he could get her away from the group. She had been a star pupil since entering his college class the previous fall. He had first noticed her as she marched across the front of the lecture hall one morning during the beginning of his lecture. She was a knockout. His mind had begun to plot out a tryst with her almost immediately. Now that they were headed off into wild, unpopulated country, he figured that his personal attention was just what Becky Thompson really needed.

The hike had been moderately vigorous but not over taxing. They camped near a small meadow on a dry, flat bench, twenty-feet or so above any water. It was the careful hiker's creed not to set camp too close to any water source in order to avoid polluting a stream or lake. They went about making dinner from Mountain House, freeze-dried prepared meals. After supper, they pulled sleeping bags out of stuff sacks and let them "loft" before night fell.

The professor took a seat next to Becky and offered her a drink of Maker's Mark from his handy stainless-steel flask. She gladly accepted the whiskey and took an extra gulp after the first sip. The warmth flooded her insides immediately and encouraged her to cozy up to Klosterman. It was just what he had hoped for.

The rest of the group sat around as the professor launched into a harangue about how to treat the wilderness with respect, and how not to make foolish moves or mistakes, like the great "unwashed public" was so prone to do. He took the opportunity to encourage his protégés to push for more wildlands to be set aside from any human intrusion, save by backpacking. And to press politicians for restrictions upon wilderness travel. Only the few who actually knew how to live in the fragile environment should be allowed in. Klosterman was much impressed by his own lectures. He believed that his "wisdom" was superior to anyone else's knowledge. Therefore, he intended to instill in these acolytes a new-found fervor, to go forth and convince, by political means, other concerned people to join the movement. It was all-important to win new converts. Klosterman was convinced that mankind, left unchecked, would destroy the earth. In large part, his belief system held to a population reduction akin to genocide, against any and all "unbelievers". But he understood that that concept could not be broached in the present company. It was better left for true initiates, later, when sufficient political power could sway the backward thinking of the masses.

Most of the group began to nod off while the professor droned on about his greatness and his cause. Klosterman noted the attempts to stay awake were failing. So he stood and gave a hand to Becky to help her up. She rose and followed him to the edge of the campsite.

"How about another little nip before bed, Becky."

Oh, no thank you, Professor; I think that I have had enough for now. I am getting pretty sleepy and need to lie down before I fall down."

"Oh, I thought that you might want to go up onto that little ridge and see if we might be able to catch a glimpse of the Northern Lights. We are in the right spot for them, you know.

They might light up the sky tonight. Maybe just for a short while. What do you think?"

"I've never seen the Northern Lights; I think I can stay awake for that. Maybe we should drag the sleeping bags up the ridge to cushion the hard ground."

"That's good thinking, Becky. I'll get both of them. It will just take a minute; you can wait here."

The professor turned away before allowing his countenance to break into a sly grin. It couldn't be better, as far as he was concerned.

He and Becky climbed the narrow ridge to a flat spot about a quarter of a mile above the rest of the campers. They found a section of short grass to lay the bags on. They also found a depression in the ground that made a natural backrest. Becky quickly snuggled up to Klosterman and leaned back to look into the night sky. For his part, the professor's blood pressure was hitting new heights, as he became completely focused on slipping his arm around Becky and drawing her closer to him.

Becky had been in this kind of situation many a time and didn't waste time waiting for Klosterman to make the first move. She leaned close to him and kissed him long and deeply. That was all the professor needed. He had her clothes off in record time, and she helped him get rid of his just as quickly. They lay on the sleeping bags and began to furiously make love under the cloudless night sky. As they enjoyed each other, they became vocal in their love-making, pretty much drowning out anything but the loudest sounds from beyond their little nest. The wind came up, right in the middle of their heated fun, and blew through the trees and across the ridge. It was loud enough that they never heard a thing from the lower camp.

Chapter 18

When Becky had followed the professor uphill, the five other campers had gotten up, retired to their respective sleeping bags, and had gladly lain down. All were tired and sleepy. No one lasted longer than five minutes before they drifted off into a deep sleep.

The beasts followed the pungent scent of the humans across a shallow swale from their ridge lair. The wind picked up, but since it was blowing east to west, the scent was still riding the strong breeze, and the cats had little trouble heading right for the camp. They sneaked up toward the campsite, ever wary when there was more than one human involved. Presently, their great night vison rested upon five sleeping forms less than fifty yards away. One of the cats turned off to circle the unsuspecting campers. It was a part of their usual tactic when making ready to kill prey. When they leaped forward, there was less than ninety feet between the two killers, as they rushed the immovable forms lying in nylon sleeping bags, like sausages ready for breakfast.

The first two environmentalists met their end suddenly, without so much as a peep from either one. One of the three remaining hikers woke to the sounds of bones snapping. He raised up to see what was making the noise and looked right into the gory face of one of the monsters. His fright never really had a chance to take hold. The beast, less than five feet away, simply turned toward him and bit his head off. His body flopped around in the sleeping bag for a few seconds before lying still in death. The other cat casually walked over to the final two campers, who still slept the sleep of the dead, literally, and cut them in two with it horrendous, canine teeth. The deeds were done, and the feasting began. Wet chewing sounds mixed with bones being crunched, as the huge cats went about the business of devouring their prey. When they had finished, they picked up the two remaining carcasses in their jaws and made off toward the opposite ridge. They climbed another mile up toward the peak and found a vantage point to lay up on. Licking the blood off their paws, they soon relaxed with their full bellies and began the contented sleep of the successful hunter. The wind blew across their hideout and whistled down the ridge toward the far-off valley floor.

Klosterman and Becky were having a second erotic session, while the big cats ate their friends and fellow activists. These were the very people who would never understand the true danger posed by wild animals, the real wilderness, or the experience of being out of their own element. A college campus is a far cry from the remote Cabinet Wilderness.

After their second love making, Becky opted to stay with Klosterman at the little nest they had found. He was elated that she would spend the night with him. They snuggled up and fell off to a deep sleep, completely unaware of the horror that had befallen the others only a quarter-mile away. Their tryst had actually saved them from a similar death. The big cats had never realized that two more human morsels were lying up on the same ridge, so close to their killing field.

The saber-toothed cats slept the night out. The following morning found them lazing around their lair, like cats world-wide do when they are well fed. There was nothing to get up for, so they napped and slept for hours.

Klosterman awoke first, with a ravenous hunger. He roused Wendy and suggested that they head for the camp to get breakfast. They hadn't given a thought to the reaction of the other students when they sauntered back into the camp site. Then Wendy saw something that stopped her in her tracks. Klosterman was fixated upon breakfast and was slow to note what Wendy was looking at. In front of her lay a severed hand, a ripped, blood-soaked sleeping bag, and something green and brown that stunk to high heaven. Wendy's scream began low and slow, then ascended the scale to a high-pitched expression of terror-induced hysteria. Klosterman, for his part, began to scream, too. He jumped around in a circle to see if something was lurking nearby. What he saw made him vomit on the spot. Several parts of severed and fractured limbs and an unattached foot lay on top of two sleeping bags. Blood was everywhere.

Panic ensued, and the screaming turned to mute terror, then to crying, and finally to the panicked urge to run. Where to run was the only question in their minds, that is, what was left of their minds. Klosterman began yelling for Wendy to follow him, and off they went downhill, stumbling and straining to keep their footing on the spine of the rocky ridge. Wendy started screaming for Klosterman to slow down and not to leave her by herself on the mountain. Klosterman told her to shut the hell up and follow him, or else make her own damned way off the mountain. Wendy ran and sobbed and wailed down the ridge toward the trail head. Klosterman kept up his pace and soon outdistanced her. He could care less what befell Wendy. His only thoughts were of himself and his own safety. "Stupid bitch" could cry all she wanted, but he was getting the hell out of this friggin' country as fast as he could run. And run he did, right to the Prius. He jumped in, started the engine, and spun the tires in the dirt before he could get traction on the pavement. Ten miles down Route 56, a deputy, patrolling up from the Bull River campground, passed him going very fast the other way. Klosterman was doing eighty miles an hour on a very dangerous section of highway. It was way too fast for the roadway. The deputy swung his pickup patrol vehicle around and hit the lights and siren. He was hitting a hundred to try to close the gap between him and Klosterman. But he had to slow down on some curves and was out of sight when the Prius left the road, hit a tree at eighty, and flipped six times before landing upside down in the Bull River. When the deputy came upon the scene, only the front two tires were visible above the water's surface. He found what was left of Klosterman fifty yards beyond the tree. He had been ejected through the windshield like a human cannon ball. There was little that remained that resembled a human being, other than broken arms and legs. His head and torso were very worse for wear, after smashing through the front windshield.

"This is deputy Shannon, out on fifty-six. I am going to need an ambulance to deal with the aftermath of a high-speed crash, at mile marker nineteen. Oh, and no need for code three, but be sure to bring a body bag. We've got a wet one, in more ways than one. Be sure to call the Highway Patrol for me, would you?"

The call made, Shannon took a good look at the upside-down Prius as it floated into a bend of the river and hung up on a sand bar. He could see no other signs of life or any other bodies within the interior of the car. So he began a search of the area to make sure that someone else hadn't been ejected also. If so, that person might have lived, even though the possibility was remote.

Wendy finally stumbled onto the highway, about a mile below the parking area. She had fallen several times and ripped both knees on rocks, lacerated the palms of both hands, and likely broken a rib. She had also gashed her forehead on a dead tree limb. She was bleeding steadily, but not heavily. She, in fact, didn't even realize that she was injured. Her breathing was extremely ragged, to the point that she had become light headed and ready to faint. When she got to the highway, she collapsed against some jack pines. Her head sagged down to between her knees, and she just gave up. She couldn't run another step or walk for that matter. Her hysterical crying had left her with nothing but a few sporadic sobs and a case of the shakes.

The state patrolman, responding to dispatch, had noted the two Subaru station wagons on the side of the road. He stopped for a minute and took pictures of the obvious tire marks in the dirt shoulder that left rubber on the pavement and the road to the south. He surmised that it had probably been the car that had ended up in the river. As he rounded a sweeping curve, he noticed a woman slumped against some small pine trees at the side of the road. He pulled over and climbed out of his patrol car. She was pretty much covered in blood, breathing shallow, unable to focus or even notice when he began working on her injuries. She was certainly in shock, at a minimum, so he rendered first aid, then called dispatch. He had dispatch notify the ambulance that they needed to attend to the woman before they continued on to the crash site.

The sheriff had heard the conversations between his deputy, dispatch, and the state patrolman. The facts began to seem strange to him, when he considered where the wreck had occurred and the appearance of a lone woman on the side of the road. It was all compounded by the two Subaru's parked at the trailhead. McDougal's suspicions rose that there were other people involved in the mystery. The fact that the patrolman had reported Washington plates and that both cars had University of Washington stickers on the rear bumpers began to irritate the sheriff to no end. It was almost certainly some fool excursion into the wilderness, such a one that he had restricted a few weeks back. The sheriff told Wade Larson to meet him at the wilderness trail head as soon as possible. McDougal began to get a really bad feeling about the "whole damned thing".

Chapter 19

Janey had barely been able to get a few hours of fitful sleep since the thing had looked in her window that night. Since that event, she had invited the two waitresses to stay over in the extra bedrooms of her house. A permanent guard had been stationed by the sheriff, one with a heavy caliber gun in his hands, during the nighttime watches. No other scares had occurred. It was like nothing had happened, but she knew exactly what she had seen, and it was beyond any nightmare vision she had ever had. What a huge monstrosity the thing was. And its eyes--like nothing she could even imagine. It gave her the chills thinking of such eyes. Her stomach turned over every time she thought of that beast staring at her, just outside the glass. It could have killed everyone in the café in a moment. And, on top of that, the stupid reporter and her cameraman had suggested that she and Sally hadn't seen anything. That they were just easily-scared, silly fools living around rednecks and lumberjack jerks that wouldn't know a monster from a ground squirrel. Damn their arrogance and rudeness. One thing was for certain: they hadn't been back since the boys had hauled their asses out of her place like a couple of sacks of flour. Good riddance!

Wade Larson had spent the first three nights out at the Country Café sitting in his truck, waiting. He had a high-intensity spotlight on the truck, plus a very intense flashlight that he could hold along the forearm of the .458, if by chance he got a shot at the beast. Or more accurately, the beasts. Mandy had thrown a perfect fit when he had decided to go hunting without a backup. It was stupid to face two of them at once, but Wade didn't really think that they would come back to the café anytime soon. And they hadn't. Now this stuff out on Highway 56 had taken a sinister turn with the discovery of the injured woman and the parked cars. Something was definitely up. McDougal was already there when Wade arrived. The ambulance was parked along the shoulder with lights going, as was the sheriff's car.

"Hey, Wade, come over and listen to this." The sheriff was interviewing the injured woman while the paras worked on her. She evidently had come out of shock, since she was talking freely.

"Sheriff, I can't thank you enough for getting help for me. That bastard, Klosterman, got what he wanted last night, up on the ridge. Then, when we discovered the horrible scene at camp, he just ran off and left me. Called me a stupid bitch. What an ass! I am ashamed that I had anything to do with him. He left me there to die, but I determined to run for it, even if the running killed me. It would be better than whatever happened to my friends, that's for damned sure. What a terrible, unbelievable scene! Sheriff, I am so sorry that we broke your regulations, and now we have all paid a terrible price for our stupid, childish behavior."

Wendy broke down again and began crying quietly. She took a few sips of some bottled water and calmed down.

"Wade, Wendy just told me about her friends and what was left of them, about three miles up the trail from where the cars are parked. It has to be the cats. They have killed again. This time five people at once. This thing is spinning out of control, worse than I ever could have imagined. The cats seem to be getting used to eating humans, which is really bad news."

"Sheriff, my girlfriend, Mandy, was a zoology major in college. She studied big cats. It seems that African lions exhibit similar behavior when they turn man-eater. She told me that the man-eaters get bolder as time goes on. They find out how easy it is to take a human versus a 500-pound antelope that has horns and hooves and that knows how to use them. So they keep eating people. Our giant cats seem to have figured out the same thing. No one anywhere in this entire county is safe from these monsters. We have got to get more men and get to hunting them down."

"I already have requested that the Guard be put at our disposal, to beef up our office. We are spread too thin for a hunt like this. In a couple of days, we should have several hundred men involved in the hunt. But for the mean time, I have the helicopter on its way to pick up you and me for a quick trip up to the kill site. Maybe we can find a track or two and follow them to wherever they have laid up to sleep off their lousy feast."

"Sheriff, do you have anything larger than your AR-15 in your vehicle?"

"As a matter of fact, I do. My cousin loaned me his .375 H and H. I'm used to shooting it, too.

We have a shooting contest every Fourth of July. We use the H and H. Not quite the power of the .458 but pretty darned good in a pinch. And, Wade, we are in a helluva pinch right now."

The helicopter arrived, and Wade and McDougal climbed in for the short ride to the ridge, where the attack had occurred. They landed on a fairly level spot just above the scene of the killings. Some birds scattered when the helicopter set down but settled in again to continue to pick at what remained of five university students. Wade thought it was very little, not much for even the birds to share. The sheriff called his office and had two other deputies head out to the site with cameras, bags, recorders, and anything else they could think of to document the evidence of the attack. In the meantime, he and Larson began the hunt.

The pilot was instructed to fly up the several adjacent ridges, one by one. There was an outside chance that the beasts might still be out in the open, lazing away the afternoon since feeding so heavily the night before.

Coming down a ridge, to the west of the killing site, they suddenly saw both monsters stand up from a concealed flat, high on a ridge. The beasts were staring up at the helicopter, snarling and growling. The hair on their necks and backs stood straight up. They crouched down, ready to spring into a run. McDougal had an opportunity, and he let fly with the .375, even though the range was extreme. Wade saw one cat take a bite at its right forepaw, just before leaping off the ridge into a mature fir thicket. The other animal turned up the ridge, running at an unbelievable speed, straight into the thickest part of the forest. Wade never had a shot.

"Damn it, Wade, I wounded the bastard. I saw him bite at his paw. We had a slim chance, and I took it, but I sure wanted it to be a good hit. That will do nothing but make him more dangerous, if there is such a thing. Man, O man, did you see those things? They are giants. Never even imagined such animals existed, let alone roamed the earth. Weren't these damned things supposed to have died out a million years ago?"

"Something like that, sheriff. My opinion of expert scientists has been on a downslide ever since we began been dealing with these monsters. We have been sold a bill of goods by a lot of folks that are supposed to know how things were back then and how they are today. I have never been enamored with the "just how stories" you read in museums, or their fancy slick publications about "prehistoric monsters". After what we just saw, I think that the experts can go to hell, them and their indoctrination machines, the colleges and universities. We will have to preserve these beasts, once we get them on the ground. The scientists can come look once we've got them frozen somewhere. But first we have to kill the bastards. The size of them is stunning. Did you see how fast the second one went up the ridge. He must have been doing close to fifty miles an hour. How are we going to kill these friggin' things?"

"That is a very good question, Deputy Larson. I, for one, am scared to death by these beasts. I feel like Janey probably did after she got a look at one that night at the café. But if you tell anyone else, I'll fire your ass in a quick minute."

"Sheriff, I am as scared as you are, or Janey is, of them. But we both know that we've got it to do, so let's get about it."

"Pilot, swing this bird around to the far side of the fir thicket and see if the damned cats come out into the open. I'd sure like another chance at them with this pea shooter."

McDougal and Larson had the pilot hover over the thicket, hoping to dive the cats out, but they never moved. They hunkered down, snarled and spit, held their ground, and waited for the hated machine to leave. The helicopter had to head back to Libby when black clouds boiled over the Cabinet peaks and began to descend down the ridges, blotting out all visibility. With the rain came the darkness that the cats loved to move in. They began a round-about track that would take them off into the border country of the Idaho panhandle. There was nothing between Highway 56 and Bonners Ferry, Idaho--nothing but dark, wet forests, and hot, red meat. It was a perfect place to retreat and lay up. They knew from experience that there was plenty of wild game within that forest. Humans were easy meat, but they were also frightening when they brought their machines to bear. The helicopter had the cats on the move. It would be awhile before they ventured back into the proximity of much human traffic.

Doug had asked for another assignment from the network, and the "Queen" had reinforced his decision with a recommendation that he work around the Seattle metro area. She didn't want him to know that she wanted out, too. So she pretended to stay in Libby. But a couple of days later, she "decided" that the whole thing about monsters was a bit far-fetched. Whatever her real feelings about them were, the network bosses would never know. Actually, she wanted an assignment anywhere else but Montana--northern Idaho or any other retarded, redneck countryside. They could have their damned monsters. What had actually scared her was the treatment by the locals of Doug and herself, that night at the café. She had never had an experienced quite like that, even in foreign countries. The people of the godforsaken northwest part of Montana deserved their monster. For her part, she planned to never return. If the locals had known her thoughts, they would have put away a few six-packs in celebration of her departure. So much for the big-time network news team taking over the local turf in Kalispell.

Chapter 20

The governor had called up a contingent of the National Guard to work with the Sheriff's Office, tracking down the saber-toothed cats. The Guard had some heavy weapons at their disposal and another helicopter. It mounted mini-guns and rockets. If the cats got in its sights, there would be no tomorrow for them. The other weapons consisted of fifty caliber machine guns mounted on Humvees and a couple of wire-guided anti-tank missiles. There were about twenty-five guardsmen assigned to Sheriff McDougal.

Since that day in the helicopter with deputy Larson, McDougal hadn't heard a peep about any monsters anywhere in the vast northwest country. They seemed to have gone to ground, like they never existed in the first place. But the forensic evidence argued the opposite. The attack upon the contingent from Washington state had rocked the people of northwest

Montana, Idaho, and Washington. The news networks from all across the three states had sent teams out in hope of a story. The sheriff and his deputies, along with the governor of Montana, had been interviewed multiple times. Finally, the news teams had left.

Wendy had become a regular on the Seattle news, when her story about Klosterman hit the fan. She held forth about his cowardice and mean treatment of her and the other students. And his selfish headlong run, fearing for his own life, that brought him to such an abrupt end up against a Ponderosa pine along the Bull River. She accused him of sexual harassment and misogamy. He, of course, had no answer to her charges, which conveniently fit into the current cultural trend, especially in Seattle and its surrounding environs. After a couple of weeks, most of the interest in scary monsters waned. Other "news" which took precedence was broadcast nightly, like which Hollywood starlet was screwing which old producer or actor. The families of the dead students were left with no closure. There were no answers other than the usual meaningless platitudes and a few ridiculous shrines of teddy bears,flowers, and assorted keepsakes. Things calmed down. The focus shifted to the idealistic, idiotic leftists marching about one supposed, big deal after another. Most people went about their regular routines of working, eating, and sleeping. They watched sports or movies, worried about the next war or how to buy a bigger boat, a newer camper, a dream vacation, or an office with a corner window.

Sheriff McDougal was not one of them. He was still very damned scared, maybe more so than before. His premonitions had become much more frequent. He had begun to have nightmares about the cats. He and Wade had spent days at the range, burning powder, getting bruised by the recoil of the big guns, and plotting their next moves whenever the monsters struck again. For his part, McDougal had had it with any semblance of news or of any reporters or inquiries into his handling of the monster search. The governor had pulled the Guard out, and they were back at their respective homes and jobs. Lincoln County was on its own, once again. In actuality, the citizens of the county liked it that way. If the friggin' monsters tried again to terrorize them, they were going to fight back. Some of the survivalist's types had un-limbered their own heavy weapons, and it was an impressive arsenal for sure.

One fellow had mounted a 37-millimeter, anti-aircraft gun on his flat-bed truck. He was seen regularly driving the roads with his friend, at the ready on the gun. No one seemed to worry about the results if that cannon was unleashed. It would kill the "friggin' cats", that was for "damned sure". "Hell, yes!" Others had a scattering of Barret .50's, a couple of M-60 machine guns, and one B-40 grenade launcher. Any one of which would chop saber-toothed monsters into bite-sized pieces. Still nothing happened. People had learned not to take the sheriff's restrictions lightly. Even the tourists had avoided Lincoln county or had strictly obeyed the rules. It didn't pay not to. There were already too many dead and missing to ignore the danger.

Janey Smalley had not gotten used to the fear-filled nights, when the café was dark and no one was around to make her feel safer. She had loaded her dead husband's .338 Winchester, elk rifle. Deputy Larson had given her hands-on instructions and had helped her practice shooting. They had gone out back and shot a target tacked up against a tree at fifty yards. She was a careful shot and did well on paper. The gun was heavy, but she could handle it, if it didn't mean having to hold it too long. It never left her side now.

Mandy had preached to Wade about not having any ideas about hunting the damned things solo so many times, that Wade had gotten mad and made her swear not to bring up the subject again. He was not going off alone against two huge beasts like that. He and the sheriff were in complete agreement about any kind of monster-hunting that may come up. They would work as a team. But Wade was somewhat doubtful if the monsters would be in any mood to show themselves after the one getting wounded in the front paw. It was anybody's guess as to when they would do something overt. People were staying out of the woods now. And no one had a clue as to where the beasts had disappeared to, and very few wanted to find out.

The days turned into weeks, and no other attacks were recorded. It seemed that the big cats had retreated into a hole somewhere and were afraid to venture out to hunt humans again. Maybe the wounding of the one had put the fear into them, maybe.

Concentration upon any kind of problem or issue, being what it was in present day America, waned. Even the men with the heavy weapons quit patrolling daily and began to spend more at the many bars in Lincoln County, or in a café or restaurant, talking with their buds. Life was returning to normal.

The sheriff was feeling the pressure to re-open the wilderness accesses and the back roads into the forests and lakes for recreation. He knew better than to do it, but he also couldn't keep the public at bay when the damned monsters seemed to have given up their taste for humans. So, reluctantly, he rescinded the closures and left the public to their fun and recreation. And, like he suspected all along, nothing happened. Except that the Kalispell TV station sent out the original "little witchy" reporter to interview him about the apparent lack of success of his entire response to the killings. And, of course, the continuing threat posed by the unknown monsters roaming the northwest Montana forests. It didn't go well for the sheriff, and he cut the interview short.

Jennifer Roslin Beale had connived and cajoled her old cameraman, Ronnie, into working on the story, with a promise of better wages and a say in any choice to pursue leads that might come up. For his situation, he needed the employment if he was going to continue to live in Kalispell. He liked it there and didn't want to have to move to a big city. So he agreed to work with Jennifer again. Jennifer was so relieved that she kissed Ronnie, full on the lips. It was actually something that she had been tempted to do since first working with him. Ronnie had no idea that she was interested in him, and he still didn't. He put the kiss down to over emotionalism, after getting her story back from the clutches of the "Quigley wench". For his part, Ronnie had no notions about Jennifer. She was an obvious 'selfish bitch', intent on furthering her career at all costs, including the risking of his life whenever necessary. He harbored no romantic inclinations toward her either, no matter what kind of kiss she planted on him.

Jennifer had a plan, and it was a dangerous one. She intended to bait the creatures into trying another attack. She and Ronnie would just have to be the bait, if she was ever to get the story onto the nightly TV news. It was all-important for Ronnie to get good video of the monsters when they came in. She knew that they would have to get into their vehicle quickly or suffer the fate of all the others.

Ronnie had a pickup truck with a camper shell on it. It would be safer than the little SUV she and he had been riding in. Somehow she would have to convince Ronnie to use his truck to cruise the roads in her hopes of luring the beasts to them. She figured that Ronnie might be stand-offish, but he was a man, and, in her experience, all men were easily manipulated by promised sex or by the consummation of the real thing. She had never met a man that could resist an outright proposition from her. She "knew for certain that all of the men at the TV station wanted her" any way that they could get her. And she was certain that Ronnie would fall for her charms, like so many others had in the past, on her rise to the top. She was a pragmatist. Whatever it took was what she would do. But she did have a kind of curiosity about Ronnie. He was nice looking, clean and neat, courteous, professional, quiet, and secure. Actually, he was quite a catch, to use the fishing terms that so many women were used to in describing potential conquests. The camper shell might really come in handy, once she got him out in the woods. It was something she began to plan on.

Chapter 21

The two saber-toothed cats had been on a wide circuit of their vast patrol area for weeks. Hunting had been touch and go. For several nights they had gone to sleep with empty bellies. Because of that, they were in a foul mood as they swung around the shoulder of a mountain and descended toward a highway. Highways were potentially dangerous, but they also saw the coming and going of humans. And humans were the easiest-of-all prey to take.

There was a nice campsite up ahead, and the five bikers were ready for a halt. It had been a long ride, their butts were sore, and they were hungry--a sure incentive for pulling over. Besides, they were smack dab in the middle of the newly-declared "Home of the Forest Demon Beasts", the "Killers of the Yaak". Where else would tough-guy bikers want to camp? "Let the suckers just try something," was their attitude. "What the hell?" They were armed, and they "damned well knew what to do and how to do it". If it came to it, they would "flat out kick some monster ass".

They got their camp set amid the tall trees, growing near a small stream. The water splashed and gurgled among the rocks. It was a noisy little tributary of the Kootenai River.

The motorcycle riders had stopped earlier and picked up five six-packs of "Bud". They had a cook fire going with steaks on the grill. The smell of cooking meat wafted on the breeze that was lifting up the mountain. As darkness began to fall, the bikers popped their third beers and settled in comfortable positions around the campfire. They leaned against various backrests, boulders, and tree trunks.

"Well, boys, the things I've read about these here suspicious disappearances all center on one or two people being taken at a time.

Except for those university students and that jackass of a professor. Six people died there, but one, the professor, got it in a car crash. Seems like the sheriff thought that the other five that got the chop were all sleeping soundly, without a lookout. That was a mistake. We should set a watch for two hours each. Anybody sees or hears anything, you wake all of us, right off. I'm snuggling up to my sawed-off. I've loaded slugs and buck, in that order. I brought along my .454 Casul, too, and it goes in my sleeping bag. We'll see about this monster bullshit. I know all of the rest of you have other heavy guns along, too, so let's sleep well, until it's time for each of our watches. Then you keep your friggin' eyes wide open. An, your ears, too. These things have got to make some kind of sound if they get close. By the way, anyone on watch, do not look at the fire. It's a fool, city, geek trick. It wrecks your night vision. I'll take the first watch. Jerry, I'll wake you in two hours. Goodnight."

The saber-toothed cats were hungry. They had been lured along on the scent trail by the cooking steaks. It was one thirty in the morning when they silently approached the campsite. The fire was out. A breeze had begun blowing about five miles an hour. It was just enough to move tree limbs and stir the brush a bit to make a regular background noise. Combined with the creek sounds, the watchman's ability to hear clearly was pretty much destroyed. It was a perfect set-up for the hunters. But they needed to maintain their stealthy approach to the prey to be sure of success.

One of the bikers got up to pee. He walked to the edge of the camp and made ready. There was enough ambient light filtering down through the trees to make shadows. He was staring at a huge boulder, right across the creek from the camp. He didn't remember a big rock over there. Then the rock moved and took on the shape of a huge, short-tailed cat. It caused him to suck in his breath and let out a warning yell. The others were not sleeping soundly, so they jumped up and yelled right back.

"What the hell are you yelling about?" Willie, the lookout, saw another shape materialize into the second cat. He let fly with his Savage .45-70 lever action carbine. In fact, he was yelling and pumping shells like a fiend. Suddenly the camp was laced with gunfire from all directions. Men were screaming, and the bullets were flying.

John, the leader, cut loose with his sawed-off shotgun in an almost continuous stream of heavy lead. He hit something because it leaped up into the air and landed square on Willie as he was trying to grab his .44 handgun. It neatly severed Willie's head from his body, grabbed the carcass, and leaped into the darkness. The other cat ran right over John before he could reload. It held another one of the bikers firmly in his hideous jaws. John looked up at the monster as it ran at him. It was huge, with gigantic long fangs and covered in short, black and brown, mottled hair. The damned head looked three feet wide. Yellow-green eyes gleamed in the horrible face. Both monsters climbed the far ridge of the mountain and were gone into the night. Two of their friends were dead and gone, surely to be eaten by the cats. Of the other three, John had several broken ribs and a severe cut alongside of his head. Tom Boulger had a bullet wound in his thigh, and it was pumping blood like mad. Jim Maloney got a tourniquet in place, and the bleeding finally stopped. It didn't appear that Tom's leg was broken.

There were three of them left. Maloney was the only one not wounded. He didn't think that the other two would be able to straddle their bikes and ride, and he said so.

"Son of a bitch, Jim, we've been hit by two of those two damned things. Did you guys see what happened to Willie? Damned thing took his head off like it was a bottle cap. I may not be able to ride my Hog, but I am sure as hell going to try. I ain't staying in these nightmare woods for nobody. Let's get the hell outa here right now. I know our other two friends are dead for sure, and we are liable to be, if we don't saddle up and ride out right now."

Jim, Tom, and John started up their Harleys and roared out into the night, riding like demons, headed for Libby. They had a tale to tell to the sheriff and anyone else who would listen. And two of them needed some serious medical attention. They rode as if the cats were following right on their rear tires. Luckily for them, the cats had stopped to savor the other two men they had carried off.

One of the cats had been wounded by the gunfire from the Savage .45-70. It had two slugs in it, one in the muscle of the front shoulder and the other in the ribs along the right side. Neither wound amounted to much of anything. The massive muscle of the shoulder and the iron-hard ribs had deflected both bullets and rendered them useless. The pain was bothering the beast to some extent. It couldn't run across the ridges and slopes for miles like it was used to. But there was no real serious damage. If anything, it made it more savage, if that was even possible. And it would become more prone to hunger as the wounds healed. All in all, the motorcycle group had done nothing but die and get beat up by "prehistoric monsters".

They rode into town and found the hospital first. Then, when the other two were being attended to, Maloney rode over to the Sheriff's Office. The sheriff himself was at his desk finishing up mounds of paper work. As soon as McDougal saw the biker, he knew that something was badly wrong. The motorcycle rider had the pale glassy-eyed look of someone that had been in a war.

"What can I do for you, mister?"

"Sheriff, we have just ridden into town, and my other two buddies are at the hospital getting fixed up. We were attacked by two giant, friggin' monster cats. They hit us about two hours ago. Sheriff, they killed two of our group and just about all three of the rest of us. I am the only one that didn't get hurt. You cannot believe what the hell these things look like. They have got to be something from outa this world. They aren't like anything I've ever heard tell about. Damned things are monstrosities. And their teeth, hell, their teeth are huge and long, like giant knives. They cut the head off of one of our friends like you would a trout. I need a drink, Sheriff. You got anything strong to drink here? The bars are closed, and I left my "Beam" back at the camp when we tore the hell outa there. And I ain't going back there, no Sir."

"Sure, partner, you take it easy." The sheriff reached into a cabinet and pulled out a bottle of "Old Grandad".

He poured a half of a glass for Maloney and sat back down in his chair.

"Why don't you take your time, calm down, and think about it. Then you can tell me the whole story, beginning with where you were camped and how it all went down. I need to make a couple of calls first; then we will talk. So take your time, and get yourself together. I'll be right back."

Chapter 22

"Jennifer, this is Ronnie. Pick up Jennifer. This is important!"

"Oh, Ronnie, I was sound asleep. What's up?"

"Get dressed. I'm on my way to your place right now. We have to get moving if you want to be on top of your story. There are new developments, so get a move on."

"OK, Ronnie, I'll be ready when you get here. This had better be good."

"Oh, it is, trust me. See you in ten minutes."

Ronnie braked hard and stopped on the driveway apron of Jennifer's house. There were two whitetail deer standing between him and the garage. A minute later, Jennifer came out the front door and climbed into Ronnie's 2004 Chevy crew cab pickup truck. He turned around and sped up the street, heading for Highway 2, west out of town. It was about 90 miles to Libby on a winding road. They had no time to waste, if they hoped to arrive while the crime/killing scene was still fresh. So Ronnie pushed it, hoping that a moose didn't decide to waltz onto the road around some blind curve. That would be a disaster.

"Jennifer, here's the deal. I couldn't sleep, so I was listening to the police band radio. It suddenly lit up with all kinds of traffic from the Sheriff's Office to deputies on patrol. There were also radio calls to off-duty deputies and the Coroner's Office. Something big is on out on Route 2, near Troy. I think it's another monster attack, from the sounds of it. There is no other reason for the sheriff to call out his off-duty deputies and then the coroner.

I know how you have been hot to get on the trail of these monsters as soon as they hit again. Well, I think that this is it. I hope you are ready, because we are going to be the first ones there, right along with the cops. It's up to you to get what you need to run with the story. I'll film anything and everything you tell me to. So let's get our plan figured out for when we arrive there."

Jennifer and Ronnie plotted their action for when they arrived at the incident scene. They knew from past experience that the sheriff's deputies, and the sheriff himself, were not pleased whenever reporters came barging into the mix. So they decided to be careful and not push their weight around. That technique had failed miserably with "Queen" Quigley and her cameraman in their dealings with the sheriff and the local rednecks.

Ronnie parked back off the highway near the entrance to the campground. Four sheriff's vehicles with lights flashing were parked helter-skelter in the campground. The coroner was busy looking at the scene. There was a black body bag lying next to a head, and nothing else. Jennifer had a sharp intake of breath when she realized that it was a head without a body attached to it. She felt like she was going to throw up but managed to keep it down, at least for the present. She walked over to the sheriff.

"Sheriff McDougal, what do you have here? I hope that you think it is important for the public to know about what has occurred, once again, in your county. And do you mind that my cameraman is recording this conversation?"

"Record all you want, Jennifer. This is definitely news, and I believe that the people of this county need to be aware that another attack by these beasts has just occurred. These animals have apparently been roaming parts of three states for the last several years. This kind of attack and the danger it poses is not unique to Lincoln County. All of the northwest corner of three states are involved as potential danger zones.

What we have here is, apparently, the deaths of two motorcycle riders that were camped with three other friends. About one thirty this morning, two huge cats with enormous teeth attacked all five of the campers. Two of them got off several shots at the murderous beasts, as they rampaged into the campground. The beasts ran over one man, causing him broken ribs and lacerations. Another man was hit by their own gunfire. Both of those individuals are in the Libby hospital. A third man, our main witness, was not injured. He saw the cats killing his two other friends before they ran off into the night with their bodies. I have a helicopter on standby, which will be in-route as soon as the sun comes up. My deputies and I will form teams of two and attempt to track down these killers, while the trail is fresh. The big cats are very stealthy and very fast. I do not know for sure, but our witness, Mr. Maloney, claims that one of the cats was hit, possibly twice. That may or may not help our efforts, but we are committed to running these beasts to ground, no matter what. I want to warn you about taking unnecessary chances while covering this story. These things are extremely dangerous. They appear to be extremely smart and very wary, also. And since they are operating as a pair, they are more than doubly dangerous. You cannot be too careful, so beware for your own good. I would like to warn our citizens, once again, to avoid any off-road travel, any recreation away from populated areas, and surely any ventures into the night. The animals like nothing better than to strike during darkness, especially against individuals or small gatherings of people. Do not allow your children out after dark, period. Thank you."

"Sheriff, what can you tell the people about these animals. No one has been able to give a complete description up to this point. Just what did your witness see when he and his friends were attacked?"

"We have an artist sketching the beasts, back in Libby. He is working with our witness, who claims to have gotten very good looks at both of the animals. But I can tell you what was described to me by Mr. Maloney. We are apparently dealing with animals right out of the history books. Or, maybe I should say, prehistoric animals right out of the Ice Age era. What Mr. Maloney described to me was a saber-toothed cat. But the thing is much bigger than any saber-toothed cat that I have ever read about. These animals are over twelve feet long and stand over six feet high at the shoulder. They are covered with a rough, black and brown, mottled coat. They have yellow or yellow-green eyes, huge broad heads, and canine teeth well over twelve inches long. Which they use with deadly efficiency. I cannot fathom the size of them, even though I took a shot at one some weeks back. I didn't have a handy frame of reference to measure the animal against. Mr. Maloney did, in the form of three Harley cruisers, a picnic table, and a couple of eight-foot tents. He got a pretty good look at the things while they did their dirty work. That is as much as I know right now. If you and your cameraman want to record this campground, feel free, but do not move anything or attempt to interfere with my deputies going about their jobs. This is a crime scene, and I want you to treat it that way, with respect."

Jennifer and Ronnie took some video of the scene, then pulled back to his truck.

"Let's go back to Troy and get some breakfast, Jennifer. We can't do much else here. Maybe you can get Wi-Fi in town and use it to send your report back to the station. It's possible that I can get the video off to the station, also.

If not, at least we can use a land line to call it in for the morning news. Let's get rolling."

Jennifer and Ronnie got their reports off to the TV station and then headed to a small greasy spoon for eggs and bacon.

"Listen, Ronnie, I think that we need to buy some food and some blankets so that we can stay out here and try to get some real footage of these animals. They must be close now. We have a chance to video something that the world believes has been extinct for tens of thousands of years. Can you imagine the coverage we will get, if and when we break this news story? Politics can go to hell, even more than it has already done. This is a real story--no bullshit, no fake news, as the president says. This is real. Ronnie you'll be famous, you'll be a star. Can you imagine? Wow! It's almost too good to believe! It is our chance to make a splash that won't fade out in three days. They will be talking about us for years. Hot damn."

"Hold on, Jennifer. You are making an awful lot of assumptions. Starting with living through such an encounter. I have noticed that these things kill almost everybody when they come for a visit. There are only a couple of people that have lived through a close encounter with the beasts. And that was due to very fortunate circumstances. I am not interested in ending up like that guy we saw, when we first arrived out there. There lay his head, neatly severed by those gigantic teeth. There wasn't a body attached, as you noticed. I saw that it turned you white, then green. What do you think would happen to us? These things eat people as a regular diet. They are smart, like the sheriff said. I am not up for suicide to get a story. Sorry, but 'hell no' to your idea."

"Oh, come on, Ronnie. You are hurting my feelings now. I know that you are a brave man. I have witnessed just that, more than once. I feel like you are not helping me, because I have been a bit of a bitch the last couple of years. I admit that I've been hard to deal with and arrogant. But I have just been trying to do my job to the best of my ability. I hope that you won't continue to hold that against me. I apologize if I have wronged you in anyway. And I promise to make it up to you in any way that I can. Can you forgive me my excesses?"

Chapter 23

Ronnie was stuck. He liked it better when she was a bitch. Now that she had apologized, he was on the spot. He couldn't just drive off and leave her there in the café, even though he wanted to. He was going to have to try her idea, even if it was for only a little bit.

"OK, Jennifer, we'll try it your way, for a while. But if the things don't show in a couple of days, we go back to town, OK? And I'm still not fond of camping out in these lousy woods. It's almost like being bait. These friggin' beasts usually eat all of the bait and anything else resembling bait. I've got a real aversion to being eaten by a prehistoric monster, a real aversion. You got that?"

"Sure, Ronnie. Look, let's get some supplies and take a walk around town. Maybe we can get some background filler. We will talk to some locals and get their take on all of it. It will make the story much more interesting. Let's do our usual thorough job and put together a really good report. That stupid arrogant wench from Seattle handled these locals in the wrong way. We can do it right. Trust me on this, OK?"

"Alright, Jennifer, you lead on. I'm your boy for two days or until the bastards eat us, whichever comes first."

They spent the better part of the day in Troy, talking to the folks. And, of course, everyone had an opinion about the beasts, the deaths, the weather, the reasons it was happening, and the astounding fact that prehistoric monsters were hanging out in the trees around Troy, Montana. It was actually very exciting. Some people were hoping that Troy might even regain some of the economy it had lost when the enviros had caused the gold mine to shut down.

Around four in the afternoon, Ronnie and Jennifer headed west out of Troy looking for a logical place where the beasts might come back down to the highway. After they passed the Yaak campground, they found a nice pull off next to a pond where the stream emptied in. There was a small grassy patch, some gold colored gravel to park on, and a few large trees scattered about. It looked ideal to Jennifer. To Ronnie it looked like a great place to have a monster show up in the middle of the night.

Jennifer had been acting coy all afternoon, and Ronnie hadn't missed a bit of it. It had surprised him at first and later had caused him some curiosity as to what she was up to. While they had been talking to people in Troy, men in particular, she had unbuttoned her shirt about four buttons down from her neck. In a sideways glance he noticed that her breasts were exposed at least halfway, and it appeared that she wasn't wearing a bra. It was a technique that some female reporters used when trying to distract men with penetrating questions. It worked wonders on the men in Troy. Jennifer had plenty of what it took to distract almost any man, anywhere. When she had it on display, no man had much of a chance. She smiled and flirted all afternoon. And she got a lot of filler material for the story. Ronnie also noticed that she hadn't buttoned up after getting back in the car, and that was unusual. Warning bells should have been going off in his mind, but he was beginning to speculate on his chances with Jennifer that night. It was something that he had considered more than once, but her abrasive attitude always rescued him from any further speculation. Today was different; his mind began to wander and to consider what might happen when they crawled into the back of his camper shell. It was beginning to excite him a bit. But he knew better, so he changed his thinking and settled on Jennifer's purposely working a scheme on him. He wasn't far from being right.

For her part, Jennifer was feeling romantic about Ronnie for a different reason. But she knew the results would be about the same, no matter how she went about a tryst. She would have Ronnie right where she wanted him. He wouldn't be able to refuse her crazy idea of using themselves to bring in the monsters. But the romantic little clearing, the remoteness of their camp, and the exciting thought of making love to Ronnie out here in the wilderness was turning her on. So, being the pragmatist that she was, she stepped out of the truck, shed her clothes, and ran and dived into the pond. It was delicious, swimming around in its very mild water. She tried to coax Ronnie into the water, but he refused. He just sat down on the tailgate and loaded his elk rifle, while keeping a wary eye on the darkening forest. Jennifer had a beautiful body, and he desired to see it all, up close and personal. But the threat of a killing machine descending upon them out of the gloomy forest had him spooked almost into ignoring her nakedness. Almost.

Jennifer slowly walked back to the truck. She had no qualms of shyness about being nude in front of any man she planned on bedding. Ronnie was transfixed, just like she expected him to be.

"It might be kind of fun to have a video of my coming out of the water and walking up to you, seated on your truck. Get your camera, Ronnie, and take video of me. I'll go back to the pond. When you are set, let me know, and I'll put on a nice little show for your new movie."

Ronnie got the camera and pushed "ON". He nodded his head, and Jennifer started an exaggerated, hip-swinging, seductive stroll to the pickup. Ronnie had his eyes focused on the incredibly sexy woman heading right for him.

The shadows somehow moved, and a black shape rushed from the trees right into his lens.

Jennifer was grabbed in the middle, and blood shot out everywhere. Her scream pierced the forest and caused Ronnie to look up from the view finder. Standing with Jennifer in it jaws was one of the monsters looking right into Ronnie's eyes. Ronnie was still running the video camera when something bumped the truck. It shook him out of his lethargy. He grabbed up the rifle and swung it in the direction of a movement to his right. There crouched a gigantic beast, right out of the worst horror movie he had ever seen. He didn't realize that he had been shooting the gun until both beasts ran off. The one with Jennifer never looked back, but the other one did. Ronnie saw a bloody spot on its head, right below the thing's left eye. He must have hit it with one of his bullets. That was probably why it ran off. He quickly jumped into the truck in a severe panic and spun out of the camp area in a cloud of dust.

Ronnie never even slowed in Troy. He blazed through town at 80 miles an hour, barely making a couple of turns and skidding around three cars that were going twenty-five. It was miles down the road to Libby, but he made it in record time. He actually T-boned the sheriff's vehicle when he slid into the county parking lot. He couldn't have cared less. Ronnie had enough presence of mind to haul his video camera into the Sheriff's Office.

The sheriff had just returned from the helicopter flight and had barely sat down, when the camera man from the Kalispell station ran right into his office, unannounced. He blurted out that his partner had been killed by a monster and that he had it all recorded on his video camera.

Ronnie pushed "PLAY" and set the camera down so that the sheriff had a clear view of the screen. There was Jennifer, naked, seductively coming back from the pond, swinging her hips, and looking right into the camera with her most alluring smile. When out of the semi-darkness came the apparition that had terrorized so many people in the county. To say that the sheriff was shocked was an under-statement. He was completely astounded by the video. First the beautiful, naked woman, obviously tempting the camera man with her seductive walk and smile, then the sudden horror of the gruesome monster, sinking his terrible, long, wicked fangs into her mid-section. She screamed with all of the intensity of the lost soul, as she began to be devoured by something so demonic-looking as to freeze the blood.

Ronnie's camera suddenly swung to the right and revealed another monster coming around the pickup truck. The video bounced and jumped when he dropped the camera and grabbed his rifle. For once, something happened right, and the camera recorded the sound and the reaction of the saber-toothed cat, as Ronnie emptied his rounds at the animal. Four shots emptied the magazine. The video showed the cat looking back at the lens with a bloody spot on its cheek. It ran off with the other one that had Jennifer in its jaws.

Both men just sat there, saying nothing. They were still there five minutes later when Wade Larson walked into the office.

"What are you guys doing, staring at the walls? You look like you've just seen a ghost."

"I wish it was a ghost, Wade. We have just seen the last seconds of Jennifer Beale. Ronnie has a video of her at their campsite that you will have to watch. I've seen enough to make me sick. I'm off for a cup of coffee. We will talk after you see what's on that camera."

Larson was shocked. He was shocked by Jennifer being nude and obviously tempting Ronnie to film her coming out of the pond. To say he was more shocked by what followed would be woefully inadequate. It was surreal, but also all too real. Larson had to admit that it was sickening, for sure. The idea that some beast could just grab a full-grown woman by the middle and casually walk off with her in its jaws struck a chord deep within him. He felt a cold chill run up his spine. These things were bordering on science fiction beasts. They didn't look real because of their size and their grotesque stature. The eyes were bad enough, but the fangs--they were terrifying. Larson found himself just sitting there, staring at the wall like the sheriff had. It was literally too much.

The sheriff came back in with a coffee mug in hand.

"Alright, men, I am about to assign teams to track these sons of bitches to ground and kill them, before they can wreak anymore destruction. Wade, call your friend that knows the locals with the heavy weapons. We need them right away. I want one of them with each of the teams going out. Let's get moving. We haven't time to get the Governor to call up the reserve again. We have to put a stop to these animals immediately. I'll see if we can borrow another helicopter from someone nearby. The chopper won't be any good until daylight, so, for right now, it will be truck patrols with the brightest lights that we can find. As soon as the rest of the deputies get here, we will assign sectors and make a comprehensive plan. Do what you can to get organized until then.

Chapter 24

They had spread out across the most likely section of county where the animals might have laid up to eat. It was in close proximity to the last attack on Highway 2. There were six teams of deputies, each with a civilian armed with a heavy, military grade weapon. Wade and his partner had drawn the guy with the B-40 grenade launcher. Wade couldn't have been happier. A B-40 was a real stopper. It was easy to handle, easy to aim and shoot, and was very compact. It turned out that Lenny and his weapon could ride with the deputies in the back seat of their pickup truck. That made it safer that riding in the bed of the pickup. That was a must when dealing with these things that came so swiftly out of the night to take a person off to a fate worse than anyone could imagine. Eaten alive by a prehistoric monster wasn't something that most Americans gave much thought to.

Wade was driving slowly, using all of his high-intensity lights on the vehicle to scan as much of the terrain as possible. He had been considering what he and other people had been calling the monsters. They couldn't actually be prehistoric, if they were actively running around the forest eating whoever they desired. They were here, on the ground right now, not in a picture and a "just how story" in some museum guide book. These things were alive and prospering, eating people right in his back yard. Therefore, they were not prehistoric. Wade had for many years doubted most of the "accepted wisdom" about the past. It just didn't add up. Now he was certain that he had been fed bullshit all along. And it was a deep and wide farce that had been fed to Americans and most of the rest of the world alike. The group think that produced and promulgated the theory of evolution as fact was a lie of mass proportions. He was presently hunting a killing machine that all of the experts, professors, and textbooks had proclaimed extinct tens of thousands of years ago. "What the hell happened, people"? As far as he was concerned, maybe what was extinct was rational thought and applied wisdom, unfettered by the prejudice of contemporaries in groups of fanatical idealists. The "accepted facts" had brainwashed many generations of students into a cultural, mental quagmire. They were, in effect, fed pablum, not encouraged to think critically, and browbeaten into accepting whatever the professor pronounced as fact. No deviation was tolerated. Any threat was dealt with quickly and, usually, loudly, bringing group condemnation upon any individual that dared to question the "sacred philosophy" of evolution. Wade had living proof that "long-dead", saber-toothed cats were alive and well and eating people. He had seen them on a high ridge from the helicopter. He had the current video of their killing Jennifer Beale and all of the forensic evidence from all of the other killings and sightings. The supposed scientific community had been very damned wrong about the cats. So what else were they wrong about?

Light was just beginning to hit the high peaks of the Cabinet Mountains. The cats had eaten their fill of Jennifer, and what remained was very little. It would be up to the scavengers to clean up the mess. Already the nutcrackers were at work on the remains. Soon vultures, magpies, eagles, and coyotes would share the final scraps of the ex-reporter.

Sheriff McDougal was bleary eyed as he slowly cruised the road. He had been pulling off at every place that had a vantage point, affording any kind of view. It made no difference whether it was up the mountains, across ridges, or into the green hell that swallowed up everything that entered its dark environs. He trained his binoculars, time and again, upon empty terrain. He was waiting for the helicopter to land a mile ahead next to the highway. He and his team of three would then begin scouring the landscape from the air. The other teams were doing much the same. They stopped at places where the animals may have left a print, looked with binoculars at anything resembling the shape of a big cat, and remained wary of shadowy nooks and crannies. Their guard was up and not about to be dropped, no matter how boring the search became. There were two killing machines out there, somewhere, and the deputies and their civilian riders did not want to give any possible advantage to the cats.

The helicopter began a systematic search of potential lairs, high on the ridges and around rock outcroppings. They had been at it for over an hour when the sheriff directed the pilot to fly more to the north. They flew over the Purcell Mountains and began a new grid pattern aimed at Clark Mountain. There were plenty of ridges, canyons, and small drainages that could hold a hundred big cats. After another hour, the pilot declared they were getting low on fuel and that they needed to fly to Troy to gas up. He began a wide swing to the south east. They crossed a rocky ridge. Below them the ground suddenly reared up, and two giant cats materialized, running full

out for the creek bottom thickets and the dark
timber.

Chapter 25

"There they are! Pilot, stay right above them! We are going to shoot these bastards!"

The sheriff bolted a shell into the .375 H and H, took aim, and squeezed the trigger. It was a close miss. In the meantime, the deputy began shooting as fast as possible, but he was just spraying the area, missing with everything. The pilot descended about a hundred feet, giving the sheriff a better angle on the cat. He squeezed off another round and hit the beast in the rear. It seemed to sag a bit, then renewed its efforts to gain the security of the forest below. McDougal fired another round and hit the animal again, this time in the mid-section of the body where it just might do some good. Then they were into the forest and running flat out for thicker cover. There wasn't an opportunity for another shot. The pilot pulled up and resumed course for Troy. They were getting very low on fuel now. He got the radio fired up and gave out the coordinates of the animals over the net, so that everyone on it heard.

Wade turned his vehicle around and proceeded toward the location called out by the pilot. He connected with the other helicopter pilot and told him to call when he was at the cats' last known location. Wade pulled off onto a forest track and proceeded as fast as possible toward the general area of the sightings. The track led to the back side of the Turner Mountain Ski Area. The going was slow. There were many downed trees and much high brush to navigate through. Luckily, Wade always had a chain saw with his tools and supplies in the pickup. Most of the deputies carried them.

Wade got a call from the helicopter pilot informing him that he was over the site where McDougal had encountered the beasts. It wasn't far off from Wade's location. He proceeded on, scraping and pushing through brush as high as the top of the cab. They were really into the thicket now.

"OK, we're very near where the sheriff got off some shots at the cats. He is sure that he hit one, twice. Once in the boiler room. So be ready, we have a wounded monster out there, and he is probably more savage than normal. And normal was bad enough."

The other deputy, Alex Manley, answered Wade.

"We are ready, Wade. I just hope ready enough. These damned things give me the creeps. After seeing that video Ronnie shot of Jennifer, I threw up."

The civilian, Lenny Turner, with the B-40, was itching for a shot at one of the cats. He had extensive combat experience with the grenade launcher during the Vietnam War. His duty had been night guard on the perimeter of the Monkey Mountain transit base at Danang. No matter how many times the VC tried to infiltrate through the wire, he and his B-40 had turned back the charges. The enemy would get high on drugs and wrap themselves in communication wire, so that parts of them would stay together if they were hit with machine gun fire. The B-40 grenade just blew them to hell, comm. wire or not. No sane person wanted anything to do with a B-40. Turner knew that no cat, big or small, would survive such a hit.

Wade expertly wound through the jungle-like vegetation. The best visibility was only about seventy-five yards, and most was far more limited.

The big cat had suffered a serious wound, but it was still mostly functional and, now, doubly dangerous. The other beast instinctively knew that his partner was hurt enough to slow them down. So he led into the thickest of the forest, and found a perfect spot to lay up. They could last out a few days without killing a thing. Between the two motorcycle riders and Jennifer, they were well-fed. The wounded one growled and fretted over his wounds. The other cat had been hit in the face by Ronnie's fusillade but had sustained only a minor wound. It was nothing that would hinder him taking apart any fool human trying to do him harm.

The sheriff, his pilot, Deputy Shannon, and Jim Yargraves, the civilian, were flying back to the spot where they had last seen the cats. Yargraves was armed with a Barret .50 caliber rifle. It was a long-range sniper weapon that was best suited for a solid rest and a quiet background. This helicopter was anything but that. But Yargraves was hoping that he could be set off somewhere on a barren ridge where he and Shannon could set up to take a long-range killing shot. He could comfortably hit out to a mile. They sighted just such a place, somewhat higher up the mountain, and, after some discussion, the pilot set them down on a barren ridge with great views. Yargraves and Shannon hauled the equipment necessary for a sniper shot out of the chopper. As soon as they were unloaded, it immediately swung up and around to begin a search of the trees below. McDougal was hoping that, by flying low over the tree tops, the noise would spook the big cats into moving into the open. They flew just above the forest in a grid pattern.

Wade had stopped the pickup when the chopper began its grid pattern. He had found a twenty-five-foot rise to park on, which gave him his best visibility so far. There were shooting lanes that stretched 150 yards in all directions. It would be best to just sit there and see if anything moved while the chopper hovered over the trees.

The saber-toothed cats were extremely agitated by the helicopters swirling overhead. As one came closer, the wounded cat began to snarl and roar at the noise. His partner crouched with ears flattened against its massive head and let out an earth-shaking roar that would put any African lion to shame.

Roaring and whipping their short tails back and forth, the cats felt trapped by the choppers. Suddenly, they bolted for more cover.

Wade and his crew had heard the tremendous roar shortly before they spotted both giant animals bolting through the trees, headed right for their truck. All three stepped out and got ready for a fight. Wade unlimbered the .458, and Alex Manley hefted his .30-378 Weatherby and loaded a shell. Lenny pushed up the sight on the B-40 and braced himself against the rail of the pickup bed.

The cats were moving at terrific speed. None of the men had ever seen an animal run that fast. It was hard to even try to follow them across the brush and forest. Wade yelled to Yargraves to drop a grenade in front of the running cats, hoping that it would slow them up for a shot. Yargraves did just that with an expert placement, right in front of the fleeing pair. They halted and looked around for their tormentors. It took only about five seconds for the cats to identify Wade and his men. But five seconds is long enough when you are already ready for a shot. The saber-toothed monsters snarled and growled and crouched for a massive spring that would launch them right at the three men blocking their way. The beasts were about 75 yards off--point blank range for the heavy weapons. But with only two seconds to spare before the cats would be on them, rending and tearing with their obscene fangs, the men had to shoot.

Wade was surprised by the bark and roar of the Weatherby as Alex Manley got off the first shot. Then Wade's .458 Winchester roared as it sent the forty-five caliber, 500-grain solid at the closest cat. Both shots were good hits, but not lethal. The cat turned a somersault in the air and landed upon his enormous feet, roaring to beat hell. The other, previously wounded animal had just started to spring toward them, when it seemed to literally come apart at the seams. The terrible B-40 had hit square on the rib cage and had blown the beast apart. Guts, ribs, and fur were flung into the air. The remains of the monster sagged into a growing pool of liquid leftovers. It was an impressive sight for the beleaguered men facing the mayhem and destruction, like what had befallen so many of their friends and neighbors.

Wade and Alex slammed the bolts of their guns into the breech and tried to aim at the remaining cat. But he had fled from view when the grenade had blown apart the other beast. They had barely caught sight of him crashing through the trees, headed for a rocky ridge that rose up out of the forest.

Wade got on the horn, describing the results of the fight down in the trees and where he guessed the fleeing animal was headed. The sheriff told the pilot to fly toward the ridge, in the hopes that he could get another chance at the remaining animal. The chopper flew just a few feet above the ridge, waiting for the animal to appear. When it did, it was as a huge black blur, reaching for the helicopter itself. The pilot yanked on the collective and banked the helicopter away from the enraged beast. But the sudden emergency maneuver caused the chopper to stall, and it crashed into the rocky ridge in a heap of aluminum, flying rotors, and screeching metal. Luckily, it did not burst into flames, saving the occupants from a sure death. All three suffered broken arms and legs, ribs, and collar bones, but they lived.

Wade had heard the terrific sound of the crash and jumped back into the pickup. He drove it as fast as it could be handled through the jungle and out onto the ridge. Smoke drifted from the wreckage not a hundred yards from his truck. Wade made his way across rocks and around a drop off to the crumpled chopper. He called the other pilot to the crash site immediately, in order to medivac the injured to the Libby hospital.

The remaining cat had continued up the ridge, away from the wrecked helicopter. The cat glared at the truck that had pulled up to the smoking chopper, and it roared at the men climbing out of the vehicle. Roaring and threatening, it stood on a flat rocky outcrop, silhouetted against the sky.

Yargraves told Shannon to call the range, which he did. The adjustment was made, and the Barret Fifty roared. A massively heavy bullet hit the cat on the point of its left shoulder. Yargraves confirmed the hit with Shannon, who had his spotting scope dialed in to sixty-power. The hit confirmed, Yargraves began to fire the semi-auto weapon every four seconds. Hit after hit scored on the cat. It crumpled to the ground and roared out defiance, as it breathed its last. The two scourges of the Yaak were dead.

Chapter 26

McDougal and his crew were transported safely to the hospital. The sheriff considered his nightmares and his premonitions over and over during the days of his recuperation. His worry about being eaten had never materialized, but the helicopter crash had come close to killing him. So there had been something to it, even if it was just the real probability of an accident striking him in his job. He decided that he could live with that. It was more reasonable than being swallowed by a "friggin'" monster.

Wade and Mandy celebrated the victory with a trip to the Whitefish Resort and a weekend in a fancy ski lodge. They had gourmet meals and a ride on the gondola, with its great views into Glacier National Park from the top of the peak. He proposed to her on the mountain, and she accepted. They set a date six weeks after their return to Libby.

For her part, Janey finally relaxed when the news came of both of the monsters' demises. Her business picked up again when the road crew returned to work. The tourist trade had increased by several fold, mainly because many of them wanted to talk to her and see the place where the animal had looked in the window.

The civilians with their heavy weapons celebrated victory and welcomed a new-found respect from their neighbors all across Lincoln County. The lame news-media ran a range of stories about the whole disaster but never really got around to explaining the impact of saber-toothed cats roaming modern day America. They passed it off as a fluke of nature. And they returned to the experts for their opinions of what had occurred and what it might mean. The same old jargon was rolled out, with emphasis placed upon a hundred and fifty years of Darwinism. Not much time was spent attempting to explain how creatures, supposedly dead for tens of thousands of years, had terrorized the people of the state. And not one person that had been interviewed or anybody that was accepted as an expert mentioned that the two cats had both been male. The obvious question was conveniently ignored by all but a few locals in and around Northwest Montana.

Most people remained happily ignorant of the ramifications of the cats' existence in modern times. Basic biology seemed to escape everyone but a very few. Those few did not have happy thoughts and did not sleep soundly at night. They never accepted any of the rote, glossed-over stock opinions and explanations offered by academia. They continued to carry in their pickups the heaviest rifle that they could fire, whenever and wherever they traveled in Lincoln County or the Idaho Panhandle. Some people claimed that they were paranoid. That was always an easy way to dismiss visceral fear. But the few who seemed to actually understand the real situation never wavered. Their thought processes were clear and logical.

Males do not produce offspring. So were there female saber-toothed cats still out there? Cats with a penchant for human flesh. Cats that could hide from modern civilization in the dank forests and lonely mountains of really wild country. Cats that were supposed to be long-dead by many thousands of years. The self-declared, scientific experts had been very wrong about two very real monsters. Monsters that had to have been born by a female.

The question begged a real answer. What about right now, the present, and the near future? Who could answer those questions with any certainty? The questions that were avoided and the answers that were not forthcoming. Not forthcoming for the present, anyway. But inconvenient answers that might be coming sooner rather than later.

Made in the USA
Monee, IL
07 May 2022